WEST OF HELL

WEIRD WESTERN HORROR STORIES

JAMES A. MOORE, R.B. WOOD, AND MICHAEL BURKE

D ARK
T IDE

BOOK 2 IN CRYSTAL LAKE'S DARK TIDE SERIES

Let the world know:
#IGotMyCLPBook!

Crystal Lake Publishing
www.CrystalLakePub.com

Copyright 2022 Crystal Lake Publishing

Join the Crystal Lake community today
on our newsletter and Patreon!

All Rights Reserved

ISBN: 978-1-957133-15-7

Cover art:
Ben Baldwin—http://www.benbaldwin.co.uk

Layout:
Lori Michelle—www.theauthorsalley.com

Edits and Proofs by:
Naching T. Kassa, Paula Limbaugh,
Joe Mynhardt, and R. Leigh Hennig

WELCOME
TO ANOTHER

CRYSTAL LAKE PUBLISHING
CREATION

Join today at www.crystallakepub.com & www.patreon.com/CLP

Subscribe to Crystal Lake Publishing's
Dark Tide series for updates, specials,
behind-the-scenes content, and a
special selection of bonus stories
- http://eepurl.com/hKVGkr

Ghost Dance

James A. Moore

EXACTLY WHAT ARE you hoping to find here, Mister Crowley?" Lucas Slate's voice was a whisper, or very close to it. He seldom spoke louder than that, and even when he did his voice was not loud.

Slate seldom had to speak loudly to be the center of attention. At well over six feet in height, with skin and hair that were as white as snow, and with his cadaverous appearance, he was usually the first person people took note of when he came on the scene.

At the moment, there was absolutely no one around to take notice of anything, except for his traveling companion, Jonathan Crowley. Crowley was as unremarkable as Lucas Slate was unusual. In a large crowd of people there was little to make Jonathan Crowley noticeable. He was of average height, with a plain face, brown hair, kept reasonably in fashion to the times, and brown eyes. It was only when he smiled that people tended to take note of him. That smile, it has been said, could shave a few years off a person's lifespan.

At the moment he was not smiling.

Slate stared around the area with half-lidded eyes and his expression remained solemnly dour. They looked down from a stony ridge, observing an area that was covered with scattered green—trees and grass, where the stone did not show like bones underneath a partially decomposed body.

The duo was currently in the foothills of the Rockies, heading slowly to the west. There was a river. There were trees and wildlife and there were, he supposed, a goodly number of Indians in the area.

They were at the very edge of an area that had been "civilized" by the settlers, but Slate had to be aware of the red men in the area, as several different groups had made clear he was not wanted around them. Mostly they just ran in fear when he showed up, but there were always a few exceptions.

"I've been told that I should be here, Mister Slate, the better to see sorcery in action."

"What sort of sorcery?"

"Apparently the type that will, if left alone, kill off every European that has dared set foot on this land."

"I hardly see anything here that would cause a great stir, Mister Crowley."

"There is seldom something to see, Mister Slate, until one looks and actually *tries* to see."

"What do you mean?" He knew the answer but couldn't stop himself from asking before it was too late.

"I mean *look*, Mister Slate. Truly look with all of your senses." Crowley shook his head, a disappointed teacher, ready to chastise his student.

"And are we no longer looking for Mister Jacobi?"

"It is the middle of the day, Mister Slate, and as we have already discovered, Mister Jacobi only travels by night." So far, the elusive Marcus Anton Jacobi had managed to remain unseen, despite their best efforts. The same could not be said for his victims, drained of blood and violently murdered.

"We have not seen him since Arizona. I have doubts we're headed in the right direction."

"Mister Slate, the lack of Jacobi or the bodies of his victims merely means that we are following a trail that is getting older at a pace that is worrisome. It has been several days since we encountered a fresh victim, that is true, but we are also in the middle of a territory that is mostly without settlements. That means it's harder for Jacobi to find the nourishment he seems to require. Even if he is not here, he will be somewhere nearby and we will surely hear of any bodies newly recovered."

Slate nodded his head and then adjusted the ribbon holding his long hair back.

"Now, back to the matter at hand, please. What do you see?"

"I see bad storm clouds coming our way, and I expect a bit of foul weather soon."

"Weather aside, what do you see, Mister Slate?"

"All I see is you, a lot of hills and trees, a river, and the four horses with riders coming up the same path we were just taking."

Crowley smiled. "You see? You found something I did not know about." That said he turned his mount around and looked back the way they'd come.

"How is it that you always find these people to talk to when I'm not around, Mister Crowley?"

Crowley observed the line of dark clouds that had caught Slate's attention and squinted into the wind. There was indeed storm weather headed their way. The land around them was dry to the point of being arid and Crowley wondered how bad the storm might be.

"There are two reasons, Mister Slate. Firstly, you tend to want to be on your own and be away from large crowds. So off you go, and they come along. Secondly, there's a certain type of person that only talks to me when I'm alone. Most of them seem to not want to be seen as suffering from madness."

Slate nodded and then checked his pistols and rifle where they waited patiently for any trouble that might come along. "Might the sort that wants to see you on your own also be the sort that would try to hunt you down and kill you, Mister Crowley?"

"I must confess it would not be the first time I found myself in that predicament."

Slate's eyes slid toward his companion and stared at him for a long moment, "And should you be preparing for that eventuality?"

"I am as prepared as I need to be, Mister Slate."

The people who came out of the woods following their trail did not look much like killers, but that was not the sort of fact that deterred either man from being at the ready. The first was the man who had spoken to Crowley earlier, a tall, thin fellow with a balding head and the largest muttonchop mustache Crowley had ever seen. It had never been a fashion he found particularly fashionable, but the enormous nose on the man's lean face seemed to almost warrant the mustache.

Next to him was a short man with thick spectacles and dark skin. He was hairy everywhere, with kinky hair, and a beard and mustache so wild as to hide a substantial portion of his face. He was as wide as he was short, and it looked like every part of him was solid muscle. Though he was dressed in good clothes, they strained to contain his body.

With these two men were two women who, near as he could tell, were twins. Both had brown hair and blue eyes. Both were dressed in light blue dresses. Both smiled nervously and looked around at Slate as if he might be slightly more dangerous than a bear. In point of fact, he was a great deal more dangerous but was not so easily riled.

The tall man rode close, nodding his head. "Is it happening yet?"

Crowley looked at him and tried to remain calm. As was so

often the case, the man speaking to him seemed to expect that he knew what was happening around them.

"Is *what* happening, my good man? You merely told me to be here to see a sorcerous event. I have seen nothing out of the ordinary at this time."

The man nodded. Coolidge was his name, Daniel Coolidge.

Coolidge pointed toward the distant hills. "Right there, Mister Crowley. Keep your attention to the west and you'll see it soon enough."

"What am I supposed to see, Mister Coolidge?"

"I can't hope to explain it. I just know it's an abomination before the eyes of the Lord."

Crowley smiled and looked the man in his eyes. "Been talking to God much?"

"Every day." The man's chest swelled with pride.

"How often does He tell you how He feels about things?" Crowley grinned.

"I beg your pardon?" The man seemed more surprised than offended.

Crowley's smile grew a bit. It was not an expression of happiness, but then it seldom was with the Hunter. He was a predator and that smile was purely predatory. "What I mean to say, sir, is that you seem very knowledgeable about what is and is not an affront to God. Has He been specifically talking to you or are you making assumptions?"

"I have read the Good Book, sir." The tall man spoke with a stiff tone and an even stiffer spine.

"Until you have spoken to God directly and He has handed you, say, a tablet with his mark on it, you should consider carefully what you claim is His word."

"Sir! I have—"

Crowley waved his words away. "This discussion is at an end unless you can produce said tablet. If not, you will not win this argument."

Before the man could say anything else, Lucas Slate leaned in his direction and moved forward on his horse, which was almost as unusual as he was. It, too, was cadaverous, and it seemed to attract flies.

"I'd not test him, sir. He is not known for his tolerance of things he finds foolish and he very obviously finds your statement foolish." Again, the man opened his mouth to speak and for the second time, Slate interrupted him. "I'd remind you that you called on Mister Crowley for his expertise. He did not come here without your request."

That shut the man up. Slate nodded amiably enough and went back to looking toward the west. The twins continued looking at Slate as if he might be hiding a second head under his top hat.

The short man who came with Muttonchops called out, "Nice as it is to hear somebody tell Dan to calm hisself down, we're here to watch the Ghost Dance. Kindly look to the west and shut your mouths for two minutes."

Crowley looked at the man for a long time and then allowed a small smile. He said to Slate, "I think I like him."

"Of course you do. He's as rude as you are."

Crowley chuckled and turned his head to the west.

He waited exactly fifteen seconds before the show began.

Dan knew what they would see. It was the same thing he'd seen the last four days in a row. Let Jonathan Crowley say what he would but as far as he was concerned the sight was an abomination in the eyes of the Lord.

The first time he'd seen anything it was just bad luck. He'd been hunting after a deer he'd hit and wounded, rather than killed. Not only did he want the meat, but he was also raised not to make an animal suffer for no reason. The deer got away. The ghosts slowed him down.

At first there was simply a distortion in the air, like the waves of heat seen rising on a truly warm day. Then came a sickly green flash, like lightning at the horizon, there and gone in an instant. The air seemed oddly blurred and then the dust began to slowly spiral up into the sky. He had seen dust devils, of course. Everyone who lived in the area had seen more than their fair share of the things, but this was different. This did not whip and writhe the same way, but instead, it crawled slowly, rising higher and higher in three perfect spirals that wrapped around each other.

By itself that was an interesting sight, but it was the ghosts that made the difference.

"There. Right there. You can see them, can't you?" He resisted the urge to touch anyone. Mister Crowley might well have hurt him. He only barely recalled the first time they met, but he remembered enough to know that Jonathan Crowley was a dangerous man. Mister Slate was worse. He had not actually been introduced to the pale apparition, but he had seen him in action when the albino had met another white-skinned monster and the two fought. Bartholomew Hardwood would not tolerate the notion of being interrupted, not after he had finally convinced Bart to come here and see what was to be seen, and the twins, Henrietta and Wilhelmina—Hank and Will to those who knew them—were far too busy staring at Lucas Slate for him to touch. They'd likely scream their heads off if anyone tried. Nice girls, but a mite on the excitable side.

So he touched no one and he watched.

They rose from the ground, lifting slowly into the air, shape after shape, each stamping their feet, their bodies bent as they writhed and contorted themselves in ways that must surely be meant to entice pure people to do evil things. They were male and female alike. He had seen Indians dance that way once, but he'd been suffering from a fever at the time and though he remembered the dance well enough, there was some doubt as to whether or not what he remembered had ever happened in the first place.

Still, the shapes looked like the people he'd seen before in that fever, and they were dressed in the sorts of attire he expected from the savages. There were feathers and pieces that looked made of bone and rawhide, and some of them carried weapons in their hands.

And they were not completely there. If one tried hard enough, one could see through their bodies.

Crowley said nothing, but watched the shapes as they moved. Not far from him the gaunt albino watched as well, his eyes locked on the spectacle. The twins actually looked away from Slate long enough to make several nervous sounds as they stared, fascinated by the dance.

Bart shook his head but said nothing. He stared, his eyes wide, and mouth hanging open, and his hand moved to the cross he wore around his neck, clutching tightly at the shape.

The figures continued rising, moving in a wider and wider circle, soundlessly dancing across the sky as they ascended.

Then the dust fell from the sky, simply dropped as if the wind carrying it had died, and the ghostly images disappeared at the same time. The hairs on his arms and at his nape stood on end, and Dan shivered in the mild heat of the day.

"Do you see, Mister Crowley?"

Crowley nodded. "I do. But what was it I was seeing, Mister Coolidge?"

"Surely those were devils!"

"They did not look like any devils I have seen before."

"And have you seen many devils, sir?"

Crowley smiled. "Oh, I have seen my share."

That was not, if the truth had to be stated, what Dan had expected as an answer.

Bart spoke up. "They didn't look like devils. They looked like Indians." He paused a moment. "I don't think that they're at all the same thing, Dan."

"Mister Slate, what did you observe?" Crowley didn't even bother looking at his companion. He was still focused on the area where the dust had swirled, and the shapes had danced.

Slate looked at his companion. "Looked like Indians dancing in the sky."

"And what are you going to do about those damned things?" Dan spoke softly enough that Slate wondered for a moment if he were being mocked. There was a part of him, decidedly not the part he cared to think of as his mind or heart, but rather as the Skinwalker's seed inside of him, that seethed at the notion. He pushed that feeling down as quickly as he could.

Crowley frowned. "What did you want me to do about them?"

"Well, as you hunt these sorts of things I thought you might want to see them destroyed."

"Be specific, please. What do you want me to do about them? What are you asking me to do?"

"Stop them!" Why was the man being so damnably stubborn?

Crowley sighed and replied, "Stop them from doing what, exactly? Dancing?"

"Well, whatever it is they're doing." The man's long face was doubtful now. He wasn't quite sure how to answer the question.

"I don't hunt down things just because I can or even just because you've asked." Crowley was staring at the man and smiling, which only made him even more uncomfortable.

"So how about you tell me how this works then, Mister

Crowley. What is it you do, exactly?" Bart scowled as he spoke, and stared hard at Crowley.

Lucas Slate almost warned the man, but instead kept his peace and watched the event play out.

Crowley smiled. "I hunt monsters."

"And are there a lot of them?"

"More than you could ever imagine."

"I might be a negro, sir, I might even be an uneducated ex-slave, but I know how to read, and I can perform mathematical equations. I can count pretty damned high, too."

Crowley looked at the man. "And?"

"I can imagine a very high number, sir."

"Mister Slate, do you care to explain to this gentleman what we have encountered in the time you've known me?"

Slate sighed. "If I must." He took off his top hat and considered the situation for a moment before squinting toward the setting sun. "Let's see. There've been walking dead things. More than once, I might add. I was obliged to bury the same corpses on several occasions, and they did not get easier to bury as they rotted. Werewolves. Those were unpleasant. There was the train thing. Ghost train, I suppose you'd call it?"

Bart was looking his way and his eyes grew wider as Slate talked. "There was some sort of a, well, I suppose you'd call it a demon. Had no face and on the inside, it was filled with the largest bug I ever did see. It had laid eggs, as I recall. And it lived in a church that wasn't really a building at all, but some sort of malignant spirit made flesh. There was the scarecrow thing. I handled that, but it was mighty unpleasant. I believe you said that was some sort of simulacrum. Did I mention the werewolves? Yes? There were these creatures called Kachinas. I understand they're some sort of gods to some of the Indian tribes. Ghosts. Plenty of those. Turns out they're fairly common. A giant horse-eating worm. The flying snakes. Some sort of creature that was part owl. Snake men. There was the bear thing. There was the dead man who was drinking blood, but he got away. Jacobi was the name as I recall. Oh, and Skinwalkers, which as I understand it are Indian witch doctors."

Crowley nodded his head. "And how long have we known each other, Mister Slate?"

"Slightly less than sixteen months, I do believe."

Crowley looked to the short man and crossed his arms. "I am a great deal older than I look. Mostly I haven't had a long stretch of time without some sort of thing coming to cause me troubles."

Dan asked, "What was the creature you encountered in Silver Springs, Mister Slate?"

"That was one of the Skinwalkers, sir."

He could see the man weighing the risk of asking him the question. He could see it, but he did not help the man along. Some questions have to be asked.

"Sir, are you a Skinwalker?"

"Near as we can tell, yes I am."

Oh, how the ladies backed their horses away at that notion.

Dan stared at him. Bart glared.

The ladies nearly wept and one of them turned her horse, ready to bolt down the road.

Bart's hand moved toward the rifle on the side of his saddle.

Lucas Slate shook his head. "Should your hand touch that rifle, sir, I will be obliged to defend myself."

By the time he'd finished speaking Crowley's Peacemaker was aimed at Bart. "Keep your weapon where it is, or I'll shoot your eyes out of your head."

Bart lifted both of his hands up to the height of his shoulders and nodded.

Crowley continued, "If Mister Slate were a problem, I'd have put him down by now. He is under my protection until such time as I decide whether or not he is a threat to those around him."

Bart said, "Why would you protect him?"

"Same reason I'd protect you, sir. His skin color and appearance do not mean he is evil. I have heard no less than four men claim that the color of your skin marks you as a descendant of Cain. That's foolishness. I don't much like fools."

Bart thought for a moment and then nodded his head. "Fair enough."

"Now then, again. What exactly do you want me to do, Mister Coolidge?"

The tall man looked at him and frowned.

Moses Blake was not a happy man. He had little reason for joy in his life as his family was all dead and his friends along with them. In his time he had been a slave and he had been a farmer. Somewhere between the two, he had been a Buffalo Soldier and a damned fine marksman.

These days, he wasn't quite sure what he was supposed to be, but happy wasn't a part of the equation, near as he could figure.

He was riding toward a town called Hampton because it was said that there was a woman there who could grant wishes if the price was right. He intended to find out the right price and fix his world once and for all.

It wasn't much of a town, really. He could see that from half a mile away. There were several buildings, and there looked to be some attempts at farming nearby, but the only thing that stood out clearly was the single church with a steeple that aimed for the sky. The whole thing painted white, and very nearly shining in the sunlight.

There were no clouds in the sky, though he knew the horizon behind him was black as midnight with storm clouds. He wore a hat to keep the damnable glare from his eyes.

The horse under him was large and gentle. He liked it just fine. His hand patted the mare's neck and he leaned in closer to the face of the beast. "You're a good girl. Keep calm and we'll get along." She made a small noise in reply.

He said that to the animal at least once a day. Sometimes it was the only time he heard a human voice and he was okay with that. Near as he could figure, most humans lied. Those that didn't had trouble surviving.

Moses rode into the small town well before sunset and looked at the people staring his way. There were several and most of them were white. He didn't hold that against them, but he also wouldn't tolerate them holding his skin tone as a reason for him to be put down. He was technically wanted in a few towns now as a result of that attitude. He hadn't killed anyone, but he had beaten several men severely.

The skin at his throat itched and he scratched at it absently, feeling the thick scar that he could not remember getting. There was a span of time missing from him and try though he might he could not remember what happened. One minute he was in Carson's Point, Colorado, and the next recollection he had was waking up in a field, not far from the burned out remains of

Carson's Point. There was a strong chance that he had died. He knew this simply because he knew his heart didn't beat in his chest, and though he sometimes ate food he was never hungry, never thirsty. He wouldn't have been at all surprised if his flesh started rotting but so far it had not.

His eyes scanned the buildings and he saw a small hut set next to a much larger structure with a sign that said Lansing's Mercantile. According to the man who told him of the place, that would be where he would find the woman he needed to speak to. Her name was Alma Flannery, and she was a mulatto, from what he'd heard. For that reason, there was a real chance she would deal with him fairly.

Not a promise of that, of course. Just a possibility.

He climbed from his horse and hitched her to the post outside the building. There wasn't anything worth taking in his saddlebags, but he made sure to take his weapons. A man had to be careful, as he had long since learned.

The door to the building was closed, and so he knocked. Almost a full minute went by before the door was opened by a woman who was short and slight with an explosion of reddish-brown hair that she did her best to contain in a large tail tied with blue lace. He smiled at her, fully expecting that her mother would be the woman he wanted to see. "Beg pardon, miss, but I'm looking for Alma Flannery."

"I'm her."

Moses considered that for a moment and nodded his head. "Then you would be who I am here to see."

She looked at him and nodded. "And how can I help you, Mister Blake?"

He would have recalled saying his name. He most assuredly had not.

"I am told you can make wishes come true. For a price."

"I have certain abilities. But you should not expect me to perform miracles. That is not my purview."

"What would you call what you do?"

"Witchcraft."

"Indeed?"

He looked over his shoulder to see if anyone at all was paying attention to them. Even in the age of locomotives and repeating revolvers, there were a goodly number who frowned on the notion of sorcery and magic. No one at all noticed. That suited his desires very well.

"I want to be with my family again. I want them back. Can you manage that?"

Alma Flannery looked at him. Her eyes were dark blue, her hair had curls aplenty. Her face was pleasing enough, but she held no hope of taking Loretta from his mind and heart.

Her hand reached up and almost touched his face. "You've been hurting a very long time now."

"Most of a year is all, but it feels a goodly while longer, ma'am."

"I can help you, but there is a cost."

"I've seventy-three dollars and twelve cents to my name. Tell me how much more you need and I'll get it."

Her smile was not unkind.

"I do not need for money. I need for services rendered."

"Then simply tell me what it is I need to do, and I will do it."

"Don't be too quick to make that offer. I might well ask that you murder a man and then you're stuck with that bargain."

"I'll do what needs doing to be with Loretta again." He shrugged. "I can't imagine the price will be light."

"There is a man causing grief to my works. I would see him stopped. If killing is what is required, then kill him. If it can be done without bloodshed, then that is just as well." She looked into his eyes. "The less who know of me, the happier I am."

He nodded. "Tell me his name and where I might find him."

The woman spoke and Moses Blake listened.

Hampton was not an impressive town. It barely qualified as a town, really, but there were farms around it and they needed a place to sell their wares, and the rumors of a railroad track coming through the area in the near future were enough to guarantee a growing population.

To the latter, there were a few structures being built, though none of those were particularly impressive, either.

To hear Dan Coolidge talking you'd have thought the small town very close to paradise.

That made him a dunce in Crowley's eyes.

Slate rode next to him, his hat low over his brows, and his face as hidden from the sun as he could manage. That the sun was almost set hardly seemed to matter to him.

Not for the first time he considered his companion and just exactly what the man was becoming. He seemed to have dominance over the thing inside of him. That was important.

The women riding with them continued to stare at Lucas Slate, their eyes wide and their breaths catching. If he hadn't known better he'd have thought they were attracted to the man.

"They're still staring, aren't they?"

"Indeed they are, Mister Slate."

"This is really rather tiresome, I must say."

"And shall I correct them for you, Mister Slate? Or do you plan to handle it yourself?"

Slate sighed and turned toward the twins. "Ladies, you seem fascinated by me. I would find myself flattered if I thought the matter was one of attraction, but I know better." One of the two had the good sense to blush and look away, but the other one continued staring, her mouth agape.

"My point, madam, is that if you have a question I will do my best to answer it, but if you simply feel the need to stare at me, I will take offense. I do not like being ogled."

Dan started to say something, and Bart shook his head. Bart could understand the problem and Dan very obviously could not.

"I beg your pardon, sir. My name is Wilhelmina. My friends call me Will for short." She blushed now, as Slate stared back, his eyes focused on hers with an unsettling intensity.

Instead of answering her, he merely nodded for her to continue. "My sister and me, we have a great curiosity over the unnatural, and we wanted to see these so-called ghost dancers. We did not expect to meet you, but that you are far removed from the norm is obvious. I. That is, *we* did not mean to stare, but you are rather like a flame and we are the moths."

Crowley covered his mouth and coughed into his hand to avoid laughing. He had seen many a woman over the years who admired actors and performers to the point of embarrassing themselves, men too, for that matter, but never had he seen anyone so stricken by Mister Slate.

"Well, if you have questions, kindly ask them. I find I do not like being stared at." He looked at the woman more closely. "It is not a sensation that has ever ended well for me."

The woman blushed and nodded her head. "I do apologize, sir, I never meant to make you uncomfortable."

Slate said nothing and after a moment the woman cleared her throat and continued. "Have you always been that pale, Mister Slate?"

"I have indeed. I am an albino, though I expect if I were truly corrupted and a Skinwalker I would have turned just as pale."

"Do you feel any different than before you were changed?"

"I feel taller. Also, there is a song in my head that will not go away. No matter how hard I try to ignore it, that song is always there."

"What happened to your horse?"

That was the other sister.

Slate looked her way. "And your name would be?"

"I must apologize for my poor manners. I am Henrietta. Most around these parts just call me Hank if they know me."

"Well, Hank, my horse was bit by a rattler a while back and was dying. I performed magic on him to keep him with me. He has changed a mite in appearance since then, but he still behaves and he is less skittish than he was." He paused a moment. "The flies are a bit more numerous, I fear."

"How did you know to perform magic?"

Slate's eyes looked away from the woman and his gaunt face grew anxious. "That was the song I spoke of. It told me what to do. Not with words, as such, but it conveyed what I needed to do just the same."

Hank looked around and then asked, "If I gave you a musical instrument could you play the notes of that song for me?"

Crowley coughed into his hand and shook his head. "While I expect he could, I would ask him not to. There's too much about this song of his that we do not know and playing any part of it could very well summon things we'd rather not consider."

Hank frowned. "What sort of things?"

Crowley smiled and watched the woman flinch a bit. His smile often had that effect on people. "Things that would kill you as soon as look at you. Things that would make your 'ghost dancers' seem like a pretty sunset."

Lucas Slate looked to the woman and nodded. "I fear Mister Crowley is usually right in these circumstances. Besides which, I never did learn to play an instrument."

Hank looked disappointed.

Night was falling and the sun was almost gone.

The bullet that caught Lucas Slate in the neck came without warning. One moment he seemed fine and the next he flipped backward off his horse and smashed into the ground. His hands hadn't even reached the wound before he landed, and only after the fall did Crowley hear the sound of the weapon's report. It took him three seconds to find the position of the shooter. The town was in sight, yes, but on one of the farthest buildings he could just see the small puff of smoke that escaped the weapon, and only that discharge allowed him to notice the man lying on the rooftop, prone and taking careful aim.

By the time he started to call out a warning, the twins had dropped from their horses, both of them wide-eyed and ready to scream. Dan was looking around with panic in his eyes, and Bart was ducking down on his horse. That left two easily visible targets and Crowley was lucky.

The bullet came for Dan and blew half of his face away.

Crowley dropped from his horse and crouched low, his hat falling to the ground. "Mister Slate! Are you well, sir?"

Slate coughed blood and rolled on the ground. His horse, the undead thing that he rode, remained perfectly calm.

No more shots were fired.

"What in the name of God?" That was one of the twins. He had no idea which one.

"We have a rifleman on one of the buildings. Looks to be using a buffalo rifle if I had to guess." He looked at the women and then to Bart. "Stay down. I'm going to do what I can. Look after my friend. He's not easy to kill, but I'd have him protected for the present moment."

Friend. That term would surely haunt him. Still, he had no time. He ran, leaving his hat in the dust as he made his way down the main stretch of road into the miserable little town.

The mercantile slipped past on his right. A woman stared out the front door of the shack next to that building, otherwise the street seemed empty. No, they were there, but most people were hiding themselves away from any possible gunfire.

The woman in the doorway seemed far too calm for Crowley's liking. It wasn't that she was in shock, or particularly curious about what was going on. No, she was calm and looking right at him as he moved past.

And that was enough for him.

Without a second thought, he spun on his heel and ran back the way he'd come. Now she looked shocked. Oh, my, yes. Now she seemed very surprised indeed.

"I think you'll be coming with me."

His hand reached for her thin wrist and caught it before she could pull away.

"Take your hands from me!" She had an accent that he could not place. There were many, many places in the New World that he had not seen, and many languages and dialects he did not know, that was one of the reasons he'd come here. Still, he had to pay attention to those differences.

"Near as I can figure you are part of the reason an associate of mine is dying. That means you're coming with me." She fought and tried to pull her arm away but soon discovered exactly how strong he was. Crowley hauled her toward the last known position of the shooter and called out, "If you'd like her alive, you'll step down here right now!"

It took all of a minute for the man to show himself. He still wore his Union jacket from his time as a Buffalo Soldier. His body was heavy, and his face was lined with sorrow and worry. His beard and hair were shot with gray and his eyes locked on Crowley without looking anywhere else.

He held the rifle in his hands and aimed it casually at Crowley. "You'd do well to let her go."

"Drop that rifle and I won't break her neck." Crowley lifted the small woman completely off the ground to make his point. The heel of her boot kicked him three times in the shin and she did her best to bite his hand. Her hands flailed in an effort to catch his privates, and likely crush them into a new shape.

He hissed in her ear, "Stop it or I'll break your neck anyway. You're only good as a shield."

The rifleman sighed and shook his head. Then he set the rifle down at his feet.

"Why did you shoot at me and mine?"

"Got hired to stop one of those men from being a nuisance."

"Which one?"

"The dead one."

Crowley stared hard at the man and nodded his head. "You plan on shooting anyone else?"

He shook his head. "No sir. I'm done. Just need to collect my pay and I'll be leaving town."

"I have doubts about that." He pointed with his chin to where a man with a tin star was heading in their direction. "I expect he has doubts as well."

Crowley shook his head as the man reached for his rifle. "I wouldn't. All I have is your word that you're done shooting and I will defend myself."

"Planning on doing the same. Most folk tend to look at my kind and kill first, ask questions later." He picked up the rifle. Crowley could have shot him but chose not to. If asked why he'd have been unable to give a good reason.

Lucas Slate coughed up a wad of blood and spat it on the ground as he stood up. The people with him, those who were still alive, backed away in fright. The expression on his face was not a kind one. He was furious at being wounded.

The song he always heard was a howling scream that echoed through his entire body. His neck hurt, but even as he considered that problem, he was healing the damage. The man with him was looking his way and holding on to what was left of his associate. The taller of the two men was currently dead and didn't seem in a hurry to recover from that situation. Slate suspected he could still bring the man back but decided against it. The song wanted him to do new things, dangerous things, but he refused to listen.

The two women were looking at him. Their eyes were very wide, and they trembled.

He could have spoken, perhaps tried to calm them, but he decided against it one more time. In the distance, he could see the man who'd shot him. The math was simple enough: Crowley was over there facing off against the man and holding on to a woman who fought to be freed. He knew Crowley well enough to understand what was happening. The woman was connected to the man who'd shot him.

Slate crouched down long enough to pick up his top hat and place it where it belonged, then walked in that direction.

He didn't bother with his guns. There were more direct ways to handle the situation and he expected they'd be more satisfactory.

Crowley saw Lucas Slate heading toward them and shook his head. This was not what he wanted; this was not a good thing. This was a disaster coming his way and there was little he could do about it.

"Mister Lucas Slate is also heading here. I expect he intends to kill you."

The man with the rifle looked at the tin star and then at the albino and nodded his head. "I do not anticipate this situation working out in my favor."

The woman spoke. "You've done what needed doing and I can pay you now."

Crowley almost chuckled. She might have money on her but getting to it would be a bit of a challenge.

"I am as ready as I will ever be, and I have done your deed."

She nodded her head and said words she should not have known, words that Crowley himself had never heard uttered.

The rifleman fell back and landed on the ground hard enough that his body shook with the impact and his head made a decidedly unpleasant noise as it hit the soil.

Crowley dropped the woman and stared, very nearly mesmerized as the dead man's body decayed. He did not wither into dust, but he rotted just the same. In seconds he went from merely dead to little more than desiccated meat wrapped over bones.

He looked to the woman and held her eyes with his. "What did you just do?"

"He was already dead. He died a while back by the look of his corpse. He wanted to be with his family." She looked at the remains and sighed. "I let him go home to his family. They have been dead for some time."

The sheriff, or constable or whatever he was, walked closer and looked down at the corpse. "What the hell just happened?"

Crowley shook his head. "I assure you I have no answers for you."

The man was in his mid-forties at a guess and seemed in good enough health. Still, his eyes were wide, and his skin was pale, and he shook. That happened a lot in Crowley's experience.

The woman, he had no idea her name, but he could guess she

was powerful simply by the use of the spell she'd cast so easily, shook her head and said nothing.

Lucas Slate looked down at the dead man. He barely blinked and his thin lips warped into an angry sneer.

The tin star looked at Slate and shook his head slowly.

"I don't know who did what, but I should arrest you all and let the judge take care of it."

Slate stared venom at the man. The woman glared and her hands moved in what could only be a summoning gesture.

Crowley spoke softly and the tin star shook his head, blinked several times, and headed back the way he'd come.

It was the woman's turn to be surprised. "How did you—"

"You just had a dead man kill another man. Any way you put that, you just committed murder. I should let you hang." Crowley grinned and stepped closer to her. She shook her head and backed away. "Or I should just kill you myself and save everyone some trouble."

Slate looked from one to the other and said, "You hired that man to kill me?"

"No. I hired him to stop that fool from telling others of my business."

"You're responsible for the ghost dance?"

She looked at him for a moment and then shook her head. "No. I am responsible for containing that madness. I have no idea what it is, but I felt it a threat to life in this area."

Crowley shook his head and looked back to where Daniel Coolidge lay in the street surrounded by mourning friends and a pool of his own blood. "That man? The one dead in the street? He thought your little ghost dance was dangerous, too. He agreed with you. So you had him murdered."

She did not look at all apologetic. "He's a pig. Tried to force himself on me once."

Crowley shook his head. "Might be he deserved killing. Might be you could have taken care of the situation without his death."

"I do not much care that he's dead."

"I imagine his friends are a bit distraught just now."

She moved her hands and started to gesture. He felt the arcane powers build around her. He did not know what she knew. He had no notion of how powerful she was, but he knew that he'd be defending himself very soon if nothing changed.

He needn't have worried. Lucas Slate reached out and backhanded the woman hard enough to drop her to the ground. While she lay there Crowley crouched beside her and whispered his incantation in her ear. When he was done he lifted the woman from the ground and moved with her back toward the place where he'd found her.

By the time he got there Bart and the sisters had puzzled things out well enough to know that something had happened that they could not puzzle out. They came looking for answers.

Bart, being considerate, led their horses along. Slate thanked the man and them armed himself with pistols and rifle alike. Will was kind enough to gather Crowley's hat.

The shack the witch had come from was small but tidy. Inside there was a bed, there were three chairs and a table. Crowley set her on the bed, dropping her with as little regard as he would a stack of kindling.

One of the chairs was clean of obstacles. The other two were half-buried under books and stacks of old manuscripts. Crowley read the titles and was not surprised to find most had been old when the first Europeans had come to settle the New World.

Slate stood to his full height in the small room but was obliged to remove his hat to do so.

The twins looked at Slate and at the woman on the bed as if they might both suddenly attack. Slate did not oblige and the woman, unconscious as she was, remained in her prone position.

"What exactly happened out there, Mister Crowley?" Bart looked at the woman and then at Crowley himself.

"She had a dead man kill your friend, and then she killed the dead man."

"And how does one do that sort of thing?" He stared at the woman again.

"Some sort of witchery that I am unfamiliar with."

"And are you familiar with many sorts of witchery?"

"More than you will ever know, Mister Hardwood." He shrugged. "I am learning of more types with unsettling regularity of late."

"Do you suppose there's any chance that Dan is alive?" That was Will.

"Not likely. His face was, well, frankly most of his face and a goodly portion of his skull were lying in the dirt." Crowley shook his head. "Even if he were alive, he would certainly no longer be the man you knew."

Slate shook his head. "Indeed. And yet I have just seen him stand up."

"Truly?" Crowley looked toward Slate with a frown.

Slate nodded and scratched idly at his long white hair. "Truly. Looks like he's coming this way." Looking out the window, Crowley saw that the dead man was, indeed, walking in their direction.

"Well, this day just keeps getting more interesting, Mister Slate."

"I don't know if 'interesting' is the word I'd use, Mister Crowley."

"Dead men are killing people. Dead men are walking the streets. Feels a bit too much like Carson's Point for my comfort."

Hank looked his way. "Is that the place where the dead were rising before on you?"

"Only the most recent of them, if I'm being completely honest. It's something I have witnessed on several occasions, though I will say that was certainly the messiest of the events that I can recall."

"I don't imagine I would have trouble recalling that event, I must say." Hank shook her head and worried at her bottom lip with her teeth. Her voice held a tight note of restrained fear. All things considered, he was impressed with her calm facade.

"I find I have little trouble keeping the events separate in my mind." Slate spoke as softly as ever, and his hand rested on the butt of the pistol stuck at his side.

Crowley looked toward the woman on the bed and frowned. She was still very unconscious. He'd made certain of that much.

"He is approaching the door now Mister Crowley." Slate shook his head. "I don't believe he's here to discuss the weather."

"As most of his jaw was left in the dirt, I doubt he's here to discuss much of anything." Crowley looked around the room at the shocked and wounded expressions on the faces of the dead man's friends. "Apologies. That was beyond rude of me."

Daniel Coolidge's dead hand pushed on the door of the shack and then he moved into the room. He was very dead. That was obvious. Most of his face and a large portion of his forehead had been blown away by the shot that killed him. By rights he could not see as he had no eyes. The raw wound where his face had been offered a few teeth, and most of his tongue was present, but aside from a nasal cavity and partial eye sockets he had little to stand out as facial features. Even most of his epic mustache was gone.

Will and Hank screamed, so did Bart. The ladies retreated as far from the door as they could without actually climbing through the wall. Bart stood between them and the walking corpse.

Lucas Slate stood tall and drew both of his Army revolvers.

The dead man ignored all of them, his ruined face pointed toward Crowley and a guttural grunting noise came from his shattered mouth, spilling a tooth and clotted blood in the process.

Whatever it was the dead man tried to say, it was lost on Crowley. Coolidge's dead right hand rose up and pointed at the man, and he made another noise before collapsing to the ground.

Lucas Slate looked at Bart and said, "You see? Walking dead things. There'll be more before it's over. Mark my words."

The storm came not much later. First there was the wind, which came howling out of the north and brought dark skies with it. The arid land spat up clouds of dust to meet with the gathering gray skies, and lightning lashed across the land, splitting that darkness with forks of fire and deep blasts of thunder.

The stagecoach arrived only minutes before the storm itself and was trailed by five riders. The people on the coach made it into the hotel only moments before the rains started, and the riders were still dealing with getting their horses taken care of as the heavy drops slashed down to the ground and were sucked into the greedy soil.

The hotel was not large, having only ten rooms, and by the time the last of the riders entered, saddlebags slung over his shoulder, the last of the rooms had been filled.

He was tall and muscular, with dark straight hair and broad features. He sported a long gray duster and a hat that matched. He bore a heavy mustache but was otherwise clean-shaven. More than a few women found his features striking, though there was something about him that made many people just a little nervous.

"Sorry, mister, but I just rented the last of my rooms." The clerk didn't bother looking up as he spoke, having caught the shape of a stranger from the corner of his eye. "The way it's raining out there you might want to stand around a spell and see if this blows over but I've no rooms left to rent out."

"You're full up? Where might I find another possible room?" The man calling himself Marcus Anton Jacobi spoke calmly. He was not particularly disturbed by the lack of accommodations. To date he had never run across a situation where he could not find a room when he needed one.

The man behind the desk looked at him with wide eyes and a slightly nervous expression on his round face. "I'd try the boarding house just across the street. The rooms ain't much, but the price is good, and they don't have any bugs that I've heard of."

"Much obliged." Jacobi smiled, and the round clerk stepped back a bit more, his eyes on the teeth set in Jacobi's mouth. Those teeth didn't look quite right. There were too many of them, and they were oddly sharp.

Without another word, Jacobi turned away from the clerk and his full hotel rooms, and stepped into the worsening storm. The winds were cold and harsh, but he simply lowered his head, raised the collar on his duster, and continued on, the worst of the rain kept at bay by coat and hat alike.

There was no one else to see on the street of the small town. By rights the sane people were staying out of the hellish weather. Had he a choice Jacobi would have done the same.

He opened the door to the boarding house and was almost immediately greeted by a small boy who stared up at him as if he were the strangest sight the boy had ever seen.

Jacobi smiled, and the boy ran away screaming "Ma!" at the top of his lungs.

A minute later the lady of the house was eyeing him suspiciously and then relaxing as he asked about a room. He was in good luck, there was a room available.

Within ten minutes Jacobi was in that room and sorting the contents of his saddlebags. A deck of cards, which he set aside, and several vials of rare powder and concoctions of his own making, each carefully packed away in a small box for safe keeping. By themselves the mixtures were harmless, but under the right circumstances, they could be trouble.

When the voice came, he sighed and welcomed it as he would an old friend. "The Hunter is near. He is looking for you."

"You've told me about him before." Jacobi looked into the bag and locked eyes with what resided within it. "I still can't imagine he's that much to worry about."

"He is that and more. Don't take his abilities for granted, Marcus." "I have studied the portents, I have cast my spells, and I have spoken with the dead. The Hunter is not the biggest threat out there. I will be aware of him, however. It's not an accident that I came here."

The eyes that looked back at him glittered in the faint light of the lantern in the room. It was the only illumination aside from an occasional spear of lightning. "I have met him myself, and I am in this condition because of him."

"He has a trail to follow. Sooner or later, he will find me, and when he does, I'll be prepared for him."

"Don't get too confident. He is alive because he is dangerous."

"He is alive because he is immortal." Jacobi picked up one of his bottles and examined the contents. "I don't have to kill him to stop him and get revenge for you. I just have to find the right way to trap him."

"That's what I like about you. You're crafty."

"I've been around a few centuries. You learn new ways to think when you live long enough."

"Being dead for a few centuries can do that, too. You'd be surprised."

Samuel Whittaker was a no-nonsense sort of man. When he said he was going to do something, by God, he did it to the best of his ability. Currently that meant watching the one man in his jail cell and keeping the corpse of Blake Cordwell safe from any and all takers.

Sam was the deputy sheriff in the area and Glen Burnside, the sheriff, had given him a simple enough assignment. Albert Murphy was in jail for trying to burn down a barn, while drunk enough for three men. The owner of the barn, Bernard Scott, was not at all amused by the attempt and intended to see Murphy placed before the judge when he made it back to town. It wasn't exactly exciting, but it was enough to keep Sam paid and fed. He was just about ready to go over to the hotel and pick up a meal of stew and bread for himself and one for Al. Hardly seemed worth it to get a meal for Al, who would complain no matter what he got to eat, but it wasn't his two pennies that paid for the man. He was gonna spend an extra penny for himself though and get a nice piece of the apple pie they had on the menu. And he was going to take his time eating it, and make sure Al saw him eat it, too. The town drunk was a constant nuisance, and he intended to let the man suffer for the inconvenience.

His other charge, the corpse of Dane Cordwell, was a different matter. Cordwell, along with the rest of his gang, had been terrorizing every town they came across, robbing houses, homesteads, businesses, stagecoaches, and banks. A bounty hunter named Wayne Erikson had gotten lucky with a rifle and shot Cordwell through the heart as he was riding out of town, and Cordwell had obligingly died on the spot. The men running with him had not come back to claim the corpse. That's loyalty for you.

The money to pay the bounty had already been paid, and Erikson was gone to spend it somewhere else. The corpse had to wait for the undertaker, and he was coming from Ferguson with a casket in another day or so. Until then the sheriff kept the corpse under lock and key, because there were people who'd gladly take that body to another town to claim the bounty, and the Anderson clan, well, they just wanted souvenirs, apparently, and a few pieces of a famous dead person they could sell for profit. Used to be they just sold pictures, but these days the Andersons were getting greedy.

So Cordwell took up space in the second jail cell, wrapped in canvas to keep the flies away. At least he didn't ask for whiskey or a little tobacco whenever he was conscious. Or maybe he would have, but being dead gave the man better manners.

Chuckling at his own bad joke, Sam stood up from his comfortable chair and grabbed his hat. The rain was coming down plenty hard now, and the hat would keep the worst of it away. Besides, he thought the bowler was a damned fine fashion statement.

The hotel manager was a friend, for that reason he forgave Sam not bringing back the previous meal's plates. But he was not at all amused. Dishes cost money and having extra dishes was a luxury. Sam groveled an apology that he mostly meant and then he walked back with two new plates and cloth napkins to try to keep the food dry. Usually there were lids for the plates to keep the food fresh, but Sam hadn't taken those back with him, so there was no one to blame but himself if the bread got soggy.

The winds were kicking hard, and he was forced to run with one hand holding plates and the other clutching at the napkins to stop them from blowing away.

He practically kicked the door down when he got back to the office, rain saturating the food, his coat, and his new bowler alike. The weather was hideous, and he scowled as he entered the building.

"One of us is getting wet rolls with dinner, Al, and it ain't gonna be me."

Last he'd checked Al had been asleep, but he figured the man would want his wet dinner while it was still warm, so talking to him wouldn't cause any harm.

Al was standing in the corner of his cell, looking at the other cell, with eyes as big and round as a barn owl's. He had pissed himself and was trembling as he looked at the dead man standing up and looking him back in the eye.

Dane Cordwell was no longer wrapped in a canvas shroud. Instead, he was standing up and had his hand resting on the butt of his revolver. Damnedest thing, Sam had looked at the dead man's face earlier, but he'd never once thought to check if the corpse was armed. In hindsight, that seemed an awful mistake to make.

Dinner hit the floor.

Dane Cordwell was not a happy dead man. He looked decidedly angry.

Maybe that wouldn't have been as big a problem if Sam had thought to lock the cell door.

"Who shot me?" The voice was raspy, and a bit weak, but the dead man made up for it by looking murderously angered.

"Wasn't me, mister." Sam reached for the pistol hanging from the back of his chair. As long as he'd been deputy, he'd never once felt the need to actually sling the Colt from his hip. It simply wasn't necessary in their small town.

The pistol was exactly where he expected it to be. It was also empty of bullets. By the time he remembered that small problem, Cordwell was walking out of the unlocked cell.

He looked unsettling spry for a man who was still very obviously dead. His brown hair fell half over his forehead and trailed down past his shoulders in a thick spray, and the day or two of beard and mustache colored his lower jaw, but his dark eyes were clear enough to see and they looked sharp as could be.

"Mister, I don't want any trouble." Sam's voice shook a bit, but considering he was talking with a dead man, he didn't much care at that moment.

"You put down that gun before I decide I don't like you." Cordwell's hand slid down to settle properly on the butt of the revolver.

Al said, "He ain't dead, Sam!" His voice was very loud.

"I already don't like you. Shut up." Cordwell's eyes slid toward Al and Sam took his chance. No bullets, true enough, but he'd knock the man's fool head through the wall if he could. He took three strides forward and cocked back his pistol like a man ready to take an axe to a tree.

By the time he started his forward swing, the dead man's revolver was aimed at his face.

The weapon's report thundered in the closed-off room.

Crowley stared at the unconscious woman on the bed, and barely even flinched when the lightning lit the sky and immediately gave way to a roar of thunder. The twins did enough flinching and screaming for everyone.

Lucas Slate had found linens and wrapped the body of Daniel Coolidge as carefully as he could. Bart Hardwood watched on and tried to help where he could, but it was obvious the corpse of his dead friend was simply too much for him.

The rains were torrential, falling in heavy drops that had turned the narrow streets of the town into streams, and likely had long since flooded the river that meandered nearby.

He spoke to the woman on the bed again, in words not known to anyone else in the room, and she rose from her unnatural slumber, staring at him wide-eyed for several seconds.

She opened her mouth, and her hands started to gesture and then stopped. Whatever she almost said was lost to her and she frowned.

"That won't work. You have your abilities and I have mine." Crowley spoke softly. "I have nullified your ability to cast spells for the present time. It won't last, but it'll last long enough."

She sat up, her eyes going wider still, and shook her head. "You don't understand. You've got to stop the ghost dance."

"Why?" Crowley looked her in the eyes as he spoke, studied her, wanting to hear her answer and determine if what she said was truth, something she believed was truth, or an outright lie.

"It's evil. I can feel it."

"How very strange that I cannot." Crowley shrugged. "As a rule, I'm quite good at knowing when evil things are around me."

"When they dance, the dead dance with them."

"Lady, I ain't saying you're wrong, but Dan wasn't exactly dancing." Bart's voice was a low grumble.

Hank shook her head. "It ain't right, dead people standing up."

"What causes it?" Crowley spoke as much to himself as to anyone else. Near as he could figure the dancing specters did nothing that summoned sorcery of any sort, but the magic that Slate employed, that he had encountered in this area, was unknown to him. Even the witch he was dealing with and her books were only partially familiar. The world was a very large place and though he knew a great deal of it, there were still places that were filled with wonder and mystery alike.

"I do not know."

"How long has it been going on?"

Hank answered that on, or maybe it was Will. "Dan said it was a new thing, only for a few weeks, at most. He only saw it himself over the last five or so days."

The woman on the bed nodded and rose from her semi-prone position as thunder shattered the night again. The winds howled and the door to her shack rattled in its frame and very nearly burst in as the gale continued to blow.

Lucas Slate stood and paced, his light blue eyes shifting around the room. "The air does not feel right here. There's something amiss."

"Dead men getting up and following after us, dead men hunting down and killing live men, ghost Indians dancing in the sky. Where should we start, Mister Slate?" Crowley sighed, but he nodded, too. He felt it. It wasn't just the storm, but the air felt charged as if something worse was coming.

Will watched Slate as he paced the small room, her eyes nervous. Slate did his very best to ignore her gaze.

The woman on the bed sighed. "Something is coming. I'm not certain what."

Crowley eyed her again. "Where did you get the books, Miss Flannery?"

"I inherited the books from my father before he was killed."

"How did he die?"

"Shot in a barfight."

"Why would your father collect works like these?"

Her eyes studied him, and Crowley returned the intense stare. It wasn't that many people that tended to stare hard into his eyes and he was amused by her frank examination. "He was a scholar of sorts, studied the different religions of the world, with a special interest in the study of witchcraft."

"Is that why you decided to learn witchcraft?"

"I decided to learn, Mister Crowley. Ignorance has never been a wise way to survive in the world."

"You'd be amazed how often that is untrue." Crowley allowed himself a half-smile, and unlike so many, the woman did not flinch from the expression.

Lucas Slate let out a short bark of laughter and went back to pacing, his hands moving to his Army revolvers, resting on the butts of the weapons despite his penchant for peace.

Bart looked at the tall man and shook his head. "You're making me nervous with all of that walkin' around."

"Good," rasped the albino. "Nervous is the right frame of mind to have currently."

Crowley had no response to that. Outside the storm continued and inside the small gathering waited as patiently as they could for something that was surely coming their way.

Candles flickered in the small room, the single lantern still burned and Marcus Anton Jacobi stared into the heart of the black candle's guttering flame. The world outside barely existed for him in that moment, his concentration solely on the man he summoned to his side.

Boot heels tapped softly on the floorboards outside his

boarding room and Jacobi smiled as he looked to the closed door. When it opened Dane Cordwell stepped through the threshold, his face nearly expressionless, his eyes shining in the light from the candles throughout the room.

"Come in, my friend."

Cordwell stepped inside, water falling from his clothes, dripping onto the thin carpets

"I don't know you, 'friend.'" The dead man's voice was soft and carried no emotion.

"You will. I am the answer to your prayers."

"I shouldn't be here."

Jacobi nodded. "No. You should be dead. That's the simple truth of it."

"Not should be. I am. My heart ain't beating. I only breathe so I can talk."

"Yes, that's true enough, but you're here and I can feel what you want. You want to know who killed you. You want to pay him back for that."

Cordwell stared at him with that same placid expression, as if he'd forgotten how to be happy or angry or sad. The only sign of his fury was the anger held in his gaze.

Jacobi spoke carefully, watched the dead man's hands where they moved softly at his sides. "I can give you that. I can give you a name and guide you to the man who shot you in the back. He can be yours, but first you must handle a small matter for me."

"I want to rest. I want peace."

"You'll have that, too. This is just a brief pause, friend. This is a necessary stop on your way to peace."

Finally, that face twitched into an expression. The lips peeled back from drying gums and bared teeth that were still strong. "What do you want from me?"

"There's a man needs killing. He is harder to kill than you would think, but he is nearby, and a gun will end him like anyone else. You are good with your weapons. Kill him and you can have vengeance, or peace, or both. That is all I ask."

"All you ask." The dead man's voice softened. "You did this to me. Can you bring me back to what I was before I was killed?"

"No. You are dead, and I cannot give you life. I can only offer revenge and a time for you to have it before you rot away."

"I was to be married."

"That's done now. Your fiancé will mourn you."

"I'd see her cared for."

Jacobi nodded. "I can arrange that. I can see to her well-being if you'd like, but I cannot bring her back from the dead, same as I cannot bring you back from the dead."

"How can I know this?"

"I cannot lie to you, and I would not. There are always prices that must be paid and that is one of the prices for my abilities. I cannot lie to the dead. If we bargain, I must keep my bargain or suffer worse than any man has ever suffered."

Slowly, the dead man nodded. Dead did not matter. He heard the truth of Jacobi's words and understood the matter as simply as that. The Devil, it is said, must keep his word when bargaining for souls, and so, too, apparently, for his servants. "Then we can bargain."

Jacobi smiled. He settled himself into the only chair in his room and Cordwell stood at the door and slowly closed it. Some discussions were best handled in private.

Outside the storm raged for another hour before finally moving on, carried away by the same winds that had blown it into town. Before the sun rose the skies were clear again, and both Jacobi and Cordwell were satisfied with their negotiations.

"You ruined my sheets." The witch woman looked at the body of Daniel Coolidge and scowled. "They won't ever come clean."

"Should have thought about that before you had that man murdered." Slate looked at her and spoke softly, not the least bit worried about her ire. The wound he had taken in the throat only the day before was healed, and no sign of a scar showed. His anger over that wound was a different matter entirely.

Crowley was looking out the open door of the shack and he shook his head at the early morning light. The air was fresh and cool and sweet, but the road was a stretch of mud and water that looked in no hurry to dry out.

"Let's be away from here, Mister Slate."

"Where are we going?" Slate picked up his top hat and then grabbed his saddlebags, fully prepared to move on.

"Back to where the ghosts dance. I'd understand this mystery before we're done here."

"I think you should stop them from dancing, Mister Crowley." Bart's voice was softer than usual. The man was standing, and staring at the window, his eyes on the perfect, clear morning outside the shack. He did not look at his friend's corpse. Hank and Will had already departed, heading back to wherever they lived in the small town.

Crowley looked to the man and nodded slowly. "I have been asked to help. If I find these dancing specters are causing any sort of trouble, I'll do all within my abilities to make them stop."

"Don't know what else they could be, but trouble."

"Not every ghost is a haunting, Mister Hardwood. Some ghosts haunt a place because they are obliged to, and others haunt a place because they cannot escape. Others linger because they don't know what else to do." Crowley stepped through the threshold and into the morning glare.

"Well, what are these here ghosts doing?"

"I won't know that until I investigate further."

"What about her, and what she done?" Hardwood stared at Alma Slattery.

"There's a sheriff in your town. That's his purview not mine."

Hardwood opened his mouth to protest, but before he could, Alma Slattery cried out, "Where are my studies?" She looked around the room, which had little by way of furnishings to hide anything, and cast her gaze toward Crowley when the books did not show themselves.

"Gone. You won't be needing them."

"Those books are mine!" Her voice wavered between a demand and a begging whine.

"No, they are not, ma'am. They never belonged to you."

"I'll have them back."

Crowley smiled and this time she recoiled from his expression. "Not as long as I walk this earth, you most certainly will not." He tilted his gambler's hat and nodded. "Good day."

"What about Daniel's body?" Bart asked.

Crowley answered, "I am not a lawman, nor am I an undertaker. Have the appropriate parties handle the matter."

Slate said, "You're in a rude state of mind, Mister Crowley."

"I'm tired. I have not slept and do not foresee an early or easy day ahead of us, Mister Slate. Puts me in less of a mind to answer foolish questions. I am not a custodian here to clean up anyone's messes. I am here to remove threats of a supernatural nature. Nothing more, nothing less."

A small smile moved Slate's lips.

"Might I suggest we find breakfast?"

"We've apples. They'll do for now."

"As you say, Mister Crowley." The cadaverous man eyed a nearby building that offered hot meals for a price. "Though I find the notion of eggs, or hotcakes and bacon and coffee a bit more entertaining."

"I do hate when you win an argument, Mister Slate."

"Let's call it a tie then."

"As long as there is coffee, my good man."

"I would not be recognized. My fiancée, she has suffered enough, will suffer enough knowing that I was a criminal. She doesn't need to know me as a murderer." Cordwell's words lingered, and Jacobi considered the idea of how to handle the matter.

"A mask then?" The man's face had begun to lose some of its definition as decomposition set it. Jacobi doubted there were any around who would recognize him easily, but still.

"No. Masks can be taken away." Cordwell shook his head slowly and then reached to the whittling blade he carried at his side. "Got no pain left in me. I reckon I can make this simple."

Morning grew into afternoon and the cool of the day evaporated into a hot, humid mess. Crowley and Slate wandered the area where, near as they could figure, the ghost dancers had come from the ground on their way into the sky. There was nothing that either could see to make the area stand out. There were a few distant trees, there were tall fields of grass and scrub, and several outcroppings of rock that seemed to grow in the area with more regularity than the trees and bushes populating the spot a mile or so outside of the town proper.

"What are we looking for, Mister Crowley?"

"As I said before, any sign of the unusual."

"I have expanded my senses, touched the soil, looked for

oddities, and found nothing at all to make this land seem remarkable, sir. Do we continue this fruitless task?"

"It's hardly fruitless, Mister Slate. It is simply that it has not born fruit as yet."

"I fail to see the difference."

"We both agree this is the spot from which the images we saw in the sky were likely to arise, yes?"

"Yes, of course, sir." Slate stared at the ground before him and kicked at a stone with the toe of his boot. "There is little to see, however. The ground is not scorched or marked. There are no totems or signs of power carved into the local rocks, and I see nothing that resembles a gravesite anywhere around here."

"Might not be a grave to see, Mister Slate. Way I hear it, some of the local tribes actually cremate their dead."

"No. I believe they burn their possessions and bury the dead. They fear the dead might be jealous of their continued lives."

"And how would you know that, Mister Slate?"

Slate paused and tilted his head to the side. I don't, actually. I believe this my other talking."

"Your other?"

"The Skinwalker residing inside of me. Of course, I also believe the thing lies as often as not and I do not trust the images it is giving me."

Crowley stared long and hard at him. "How long has this thing been talking to you?"

"Not talking. Singing. It is the song I hear so often, or at least it communicates through the song. I can't explain it better than that, Mister Crowley, but I hear it constantly."

Crowley nodded slowly and said no more on the subject. "In any event, we're not that long away from when the sun starts down and the ghost dance should start again. I am not certain if this is the best place to be when that happens."

"I see no sign of damage to the area, not even a scorched leaf." Slate looked around carefully, opening his senses to everything around them, as Crowley had taught him and then schooled him about very nearly every day.

So he saw the stranger first.

"We have company, Mister Crowley." As always, he spoke softly.

The man came from the direction away from town, walking

steadily. He had no horse, or if he did, the animal was well away from them. The sun was behind him and he sported a broad-brimmed hat that left his face in shadows. He was also carrying what looked to be a twelve-gauge shotgun draped over one shoulder.

He walked toward them on a direct path. He was not off to one side or the other and near as they could tell his attention was focused on the two of them.

Crowley nodded slowly. "So it seems, Mister Slate."

"Which of us do you suppose he wants to talk to, Mister Crowley?"

"Not at all sure talking is what that man has in mind, Mister Slate."

He heard them, or at least seemed to, and the man's stride grew longer as he moved more quickly in their direction. "I do not like this in the least," Slate whispered as he wiped his hands on the vest he sported and eyed the stranger.

Crowley said nothing.

The stranger said nothing, but he stopped not far from them and his face turned slowly, first to stare at Lucas Slate, and then at Jonathan Crowley.

"Which one of you answers to Crowley?" The voice was a soft, hoarse whisper.

Crowley shook his head. "Like trying to listen to you, Mister Slate. A man has to concentrate to hear your words."

"He wants to know which of us is you."

"I heard him." Crowley sighed. "I'm Jonathan Crowley." He looked at the shotgun wielder and turned toward the man, facing him square on. His hand gestured for Slate to back away but if the albino noticed, he did not heed the gesture.

Crowley managed to dodge to the side when the shotgun came around and aimed for his chest. Heat lashed across his back and left hip, followed a second later by a lightning blast of pain and thunder.

He could barely stand. The pain was a huge weight crushing down on him, and though he knew the wound was not fatal, it stole his breath and strength alike.

Crowley rolled over and pushed himself into a sitting position, reaching with his right hand toward the pistol on his hip.

By the time he'd reoriented himself, Lucas Slate was moving

forward, one of his Army revolvers drawn, and firing at the man with the shotgun.

The stranger did not flinch or move back willingly as the first bullet hit him, but he did move. His entire body staggered as the lead caught him in his chest and blew through his ribcage, striking like a mule kick and sending him sprawling. His hat fell away and he made not a sound, not even a grunt of pain.

Slate walked closer and cocked back the hammer on his revolver, his face a cold, cadaverous mask.

"Are you well, Mister Crowley?"

The itching sensation kicked in and much as Crowley hated that feeling like fire ants crawling through his wounded flesh, he knew he was already healing from the damage he'd taken.

"I'm on the mend, sir." He gasped the words as the buckshot in his body forced itself out of the dozen or so small wounds peppering his side and back.

The man on the ground sat up abruptly and snatched his shotgun from where it had fallen in one quick move. He leveled the weapon at Lucas Slate, and quickly loaded a fresh shell, all while Slate looked toward Crowley.

"Mister Slate!"

Slate turned to the man he had shot and stopped moving as he saw the state of the shotgun wielder. The man's chest had been opened. He had a very large wound through the ribcage, large enough for Lucas Slate to see the sunlight shine through the hole left in body and clothing alike. Despite the fact that the sun was behind his enemy, Slate could also see that over half of the man's face had been carved away. The skin from around his forehead and all the way down to his nose had been cut and peeled away like the rind on a grisly orange. Bone clearly showed where eyebrows and nose should have been, and bloody trails of ruin dripped down the rest of his face. His eyes remained but aside from that, the top half of his face was a bloodied skull.

Slate stood perfectly still as he tried to absorb what he was seeing. In his time he had been an undertaker and had buried more bodies than he ever wanted to recall, but he had seldom seen a face so thoroughly mutilated and he had never seen a man survive that sort of wound. Even if he had the man would have been driven mad by the pain, surely.

While Lucas Slate considered the impossibility of the man with the ruined face, that very same man leveled the shotgun toward him. The wide bore of the shotgun stared at him like a black eye, and Slate wondered if he would survive the wound that was surely coming his way.

Crowley shot first. His aim was true, and the ruined man's aim was knocked off as he was blown sideways by the close-range bullet that tore through his side and blew another hole in his chest.

Crowley did not stop with one bullet, but fired twice more, tearing more of the man away, half removing his left arm and sending the shotgun sailing away from the man who'd employed it.

Slate shook off his paralysis and took in a shuddering breath. He had left himself open and was lucky to be alive, he knew that. He also knew the man Crowley had shot had to be dead. No one could survive that sort of trauma.

The man with the ruined face rolled over and stood up, staggered, wounded, but moving as if half of his chest was not flayed open and spilling out all that was inside of him.

"Mister Slate! Defend yourself!" Crowley's voice was harsh, but a necessary reminder that he was in a dangerous situation. Slate stepped back and aimed at the impossibly wounded man who was even now reaching for a revolver strapped at his hip. Three bullets slammed into the man. By all possible rights that should have ended him. The impacts tore at his arm, his chest, and his pelvis because Slate wanted him dead and stopped.

The man with the ruined face drew his revolver, aimed calmly, took the bullets to his body, and continued to aim not at Slate, but at Crowley.

Crowley shook his head and crawled across the ground as he tried to stand while simultaneously avoiding getting hit.

The man aimed, completely ignored the bullet Slate fired into him and shot Crowley in the hip. Crowley screamed and was knocked sideways by the impact.

Slate fired again, this time putting a bullet through the ruined face of the gunman. Slate stepped forward and aimed, pulled the trigger on an empty chamber and pulled the Army revolver on his other hip. He dropped his first revolver and switched the fresh one to his right hand, then fired again and again.

More bullets hit the dead man. His head exploded from the second round and still he stood, but he did not pull the trigger again.

Slate spat words that made no sense to either him or Crowley. It was the Skinwalker that spoke now, not the ex-undertaker. The body twitched and spasmed and shook before smoke rose from the ruined flesh and shredded clothing. A moment later flames erupted from the spasming form and it collapsed to its knees.

Crowley crawled across the ground, moving away from the corpse as it erupted into a blaze worthy of a funeral pyre, burning fiercely bright in the sunlight, and belching a heavy black smoke that quickly painted the sky. Lucas Slate moved over to him and spoke softly. "Can I be of assistance?"

"You already were." Crowley spoke past gritted teeth. "Likely I'm alive because of you."

'That man would not die." Slate looked at the ruined form.

Crowley stopped his crawl and stood up, wincing in pain. His hand pulled the edge of his pants lower as he stared at the deep wound in his hip. As both men watched the hole grew smaller, the skin unmarred by so much as a scar. Before the wound was gone the lead of the bullet forced itself from his body.

"That man was already dead. Seemed as determined to keep going as any revenant I have ever encountered."

"You have run across that sort of horror before?"

"More than once. Hard to kill a dead man, Mister Slate. And he was very dead."

"If the things we saw in Carson's Point had been that lively, I fear we would not have survived."

"I cannot believe I am saying this, but happily there is more than one type of walking dead man, and not all of them are that durable."

"I will count my blessings and hope to never meet hardier, sir."

"My questions are who sent him, and why was his face missing."

"I'd be more worried about who sent him."

"Precisely why that was my first question, Mister Slate." Crowley sighed. "And now we have company again." Crowley nodded amiably at the approaching figures. They looked down the slope leading back to where he and the rest of their group had been the day before.

Slate turned to see the sisters, Will and Hank, and Bart Hardwood with them. All three looked from Crowley to Slate lingered on the albino. "Are we too late for the ghost dance?" It was one of the sisters who asked.

Slate shook his head. "You are not." The two of them stared at him again with wide eyes. Slate squinted up at the sun. "Have a while yet, I imagine."

"There is a dead man near to you, who was not here yesterday." Bart nodded to the corpse they had done so very much damage to. "He does not appear to be completely intact."

Crowley said, "In fact he was rather lively a few minutes ago. Did you not hear the gunfire?"

"Oh, we did." Bart shook his head. "Would have been here sooner had we not."

"He was already dead, which begs the question of who or what keeps bringing the dead back around."

"Perhaps that is the purpose of these dancing ghosts?"

"I cannot say for certain, but I have my doubts. If they were the cause I cannot understand why they would have sent that particular dead man after me."

"After you?" The same sister who'd spoken before asked.

"He actually asked for Mister Crowley by name before shooting."

Bart pulled a watch from his vest pocket and stared at the time. "Might it be wise for you gentlemen to come up here before the ghost dance starts? By my reckoning we only have a few short minutes to wait."

Crowley shook his head. "I intend to watch from here to see if I can determine the source of this odd phenomenon."

"And I will join him in this endeavor." Slate looked from one sister to the other and then to Bart. That said, they all waited where they were, which was substantially closer to the source of the ghost dance than they had been the day before.

The ground not ten feet from where Lucas Slate stood pulsed with a sickly green glow that brightened to a brilliance rivaling the sun for all of three seconds, and then the specters rose from the ground on a breeze that blew from the dusty earth and carried all manner of debris with it. Up close the figures were unremarkable, save for their attire and their writhing dance. They were surely Indians, but up close it was clear they were not solid but rather phantoms—images and little more. Their mouths moved but they made no sound, their bodies danced and their feet stomped the air but none of the figures seemed to notice the people around them. They rose into the air in a spiral and for nearly two minutes they genuflected and moved to no particular rhythm, few of them in sync with each other, none of them standing out as a leader of any sort. As before, they danced and when their time was up, they simply vanished and the breeze that seemed to lift them higher faded away, and the dust and leaves and dried grass that had lifted into the air fell lazily back to earth as if drizzled from the hands that had lifted it toward the skies.

Slate frowned. "I sense nothing from them, Mister Crowley. Nothing good and nothing malevolent."

Crowley nodded his head in agreement. "There was nothing to sense, Mister Slate. There is no intent here, no maliciousness, and no good will."

Crowley frowned.

"Might as well be looking in a mirror and seeing a reflection."

"Do you intend to do anything about these ghosts, Mister Crowley?" Bart's voice rang out from above them and the man looked down the slope to where they still stood, a slight frown on his face.

"No sir, I do not."

"And why is that?"

"Because there's nothing to do. I expect that a bit of digging just there," Crowley pointed to the area where the green light had shown itself, "would reveal a collection of bones, possibly as many as twenty-five or so bodies or their remains. This is nothing but a memorial to people who died and were buried there. I do not know how, or why such a memorial exists, but it is harmless in my estimation. Should you want to remove it, you and a few associates can unearth those remains and find a new place to bury them."

"But why—-?"

Crowley cut the man off. "Because there is nothing harmful to it, my good man. I am not a custodian, nor an undertaker, as has been discussed before. I simply have no reason to care."

Will shook her head. "Are you certain?"

"No ill will has befallen either me or Mister Slate and we were standing right near where the ghosts came from the ground. They are as harmless as a cloud on a sunny day."

Crowley started up the hill, with not even a limp to show that he had ever been hurt, and Slate followed.

When they reached the top of the incline Crowley looked back at the dead man on the ground and shook his head. Slate said, "I must admit I'm rather curious as to who decided to have a dead man try to kill you."

Crowley's smile bloomed slowly, and he turned his head toward the town where they had spent the night in the witch's shack. "Oh, I've a notion or two."

"Do you, indeed?"

Crowley looked at the corpse behind him one last time. "I have a ghost down there raging and calling a name."

"And what name would that be?"

Crowley smiled. "Jacobi."

"The vampire?"

"Apparently he is something else entirely, Mister Slate."

"Indeed?"

"I do believe I'll go pay the man a visit, Mister Slate, and find out for certain."

The undertaker's wagon rested in a shady spot near the church, and the man was busy measuring the deputy's body for a coffin he had yet to build. He was a well-dressed man, with a ponderous belly, but he seemed pleasant enough. There was only one body at the moment, which was fine for him, though the way the sheriff had spoken he'd expected more than one corpse. Something about an outlaw that had been shot down only the body was missing and the only man who knew what had happened was apparently the town drunk and not very reliable.

Crowley and Slate rode past the wagon and Slate took the time to nod amiably to the man, who blanched a bit upon considering the albino.

Crowley climbed from his horse and walked into the only hotel in town, taking two minutes to discover that the man he was looking for was not staying there. By the time he was done, Lucas Slate had climbed down from his own horse and was looking around the area with mild curiosity.

His Colt Army pistols were strapped to his hips, and the longish coat he sported hid them away well enough. There were few people walking the streets of the town and those that did gave him a wide berth as if he might be an aggravated rattler looking for trouble.

Slate was here to look out for possible trouble, and that was exactly what he did.

Jonathan Crowley, on the other hand, did what he did best, and hunted. It did not take him long to find Marcus Anton Jacobi. There were only so many rooms available in the area and as the hotel was full he moved to the boarding house across the street.

Jacobi was expecting him.

The man had already repacked his belongings and had planned on leaving town. The second death of his gunslinger was not what he'd expected. It was the first time in his long experience that one of his champions had been defeated. The dead were merciless, and they were hard to stop, but Jonathan Crowley had accomplished the task and lived to tell the tale, that was all the reason Jacobi needed to leave the area as quickly as he could.

"I warned you." The voice came from the bag he carried, and he set the bag down on the narrow bed where he'd slept the morning and most of the day away, recovering from the sorceries he'd used to raise a champion from the dead and watch as his champion fought on his behalf.

"Yes, you did, and now I am heeding that warning."

"Too late. The Hunter is here for you." There was no gloating in the voice, only a distant echo of fear. "He is relentless."

Jacobi shook his head and reached into the bag, pulling out the skull that was his constant companion. The skull was wrapped in bands of leather that imitated the muscles which had once surrounded the relic. The leather connected the lower jaw with the rest of the skull, and carefully mimicked the play of muscles around the temple and face as well. Heavy jewels, clear cut and well-polished, filled the eye sockets, and in several places, screws had been placed to hold the entire collection together properly. All of the adornments were carried within a metal and glass case, just exactly large enough to hold the skull securely.

Those leather bands creaked softly as the jaw opened and the voice came out once more. "He is the Hunter. You should leave here and take me with you."

"He may be relentless, but I am not without my own abilities. I have fought others before who tried to hunt me down. I am not easy prey to stalk and hunt. I am a predator."

But even as he spoke Jacobi looked toward the door to his room and wondered where Crowley lurked. A cold dread filled him. The man had been injured, badly wounded, and now he hunted for Jacobi. Jacobi gathered his saddlebags and slipped the skull back into its bag, ready to leave the area. He paused for only a moment and prepared himself as best he could. He did not like to travel by day. He preferred the darkness but did not need it to be safe. Sunset was still an hour away.

He left the boarding house as quietly as he could and headed for the stables where his horse waited.

Not but twenty yards from the front of the boarding house, the albino was looking around. He recognized the man immediately as Crowley's companion. He had seen him, had watched the man through Cordwell's eyes when he sent his champion to kill the Hunter. Lucas Slate looked his way and said nothing as he stared at Jacobi, his face hidden in the shadows of his top hat.

Jacobi looked back and considered the Colt at his hip. He was not a gunslinger. He could fire a weapon if he had to, but he preferred sorcery to six-shooters and was better with spells than he was with bullets. But spells took time and a different sort of effort. He summoned the dead, he manipulated corpses to do his bidding, yes, but it took time and energy and the albino was looking his way with that dour expression on his too thin face.

"Mister Crowley was just looking for you, sir. I believe he took offense to your earlier actions." The tall, pale man stared hard as Jacobi lowered his bags to the ground next to him and eyed the stables so close by. One hand moved toward his hip, where a holster might well hold a weapon. Jacobi stopped moving and shook his head slowly.

"I don't know what you're talking about." His hand drifted closer to the weapon on his own left hip, and Jacobi took a slow, deep breath in preparation and to calm his nerves.

"You, sir, are a poor liar."

Jacobi shook his head. "I've no reason to lie to you."

"I believe we both know better." The albino said, moving his coat out of the way, revealing the Army pistol's handle.

The voice from his bag was clear enough for both of them to hear.

"Kill him, Marcus! Kill him now, before the other one comes back!"

Jacobi looked down toward the bag.

The albino pulled his revolver and fired at the bag without hesitation, and the bullet smashed glass. "No! What did you do?" Jacobi reached down for his bag and pulled back a second later as a second bullet hit the bag and sent it sliding through the dirt. The head he had carried with him for decades let out a shriek and then grew silent as a third bullet struck the bag with an audible crunch.

All thoughts of protecting himself left Jacobi as he reached for the bag and pulled it open, examining the ruin of the skull. The cranium was shattered, and whatever had been inside the cage of bone was gone now, released from where it had rested for so long.

"You killed him!" Jacobi's rage was a burning thing, and he glared at the albino as he approached. "I'll see you dead!"

If the gaunt man was impressed by his fury he did not show it. Instead, the pale man stepped closer and looked down at the bag and the few remains of the man who had been Jacobi's companion and instructor for over half a century

Slate's eyes moved from the bag to Jacobi, and he spoke softly, with almost no inflection. "I believe whatever was in your bag was already dead, Mister Jacobi."

"I'll see you dead, you bastard."

The other one came from the stables, walking with slow steady steps and looking at Jacobi. "Here now, what's this then?"

His mentor had said the Hunter could be killed by mundane weapons, and Jacobi listened to that advice, heeded it, and drew his revolver without another word.

Lucas Slate shot him in the head before he could aim.

"What just happened, Mister Slate?"

"I believe I just killed Marcus Jacobi."

Crowley frowned. "What is he doing here?"

"You already said he's the one who sent the dead man after you, Mister Crowley." Lucas Slate stared down at the body, making himself observe the state of the corpse, absorbing every detail. "I have killed before, but not much of what we've battled was human, Mister Crowley."

"And do you feel different for it, Mister Slate?"

"I'm not certain. I just know he was planning more mayhem."

"Jacobi might have been human, Mister Slate, but he was a killer. He ended several lives as we both know. We've followed him halfway across these territories, and found bodies wherever we went."

"What was he doing, Mister Crowley?"

"I can't say for certain, but he was a killer and if he'd been a vampire as we suspected, or if he had been a goblin of some sort, we'd have killed him." Crowley looked at his companion for a long moment. "In the end, there's not much difference between a man and a monster if the man acts the part of the monster, sir. If you had not put him down, I would have."

Slate nodded his head slowly.

"He had a talking skull in his bag. I shot that, too."

"I've never much liked necromancy."

"Necromancy?"

"Sorcery dealing with the animation of the dead, and the corruption of the spirits of the dead. Vile stuff under the best of circumstances."

Slate nodded slowly. "Seems to be a common enough theme, Mister Crowley. We've seen it more than once, I'm afraid."

"True enough." Crowley sighed. "I'm weary, Mister Slate."

"Justifiably so, sir."

Not far away Bart Hardwood and the twins rode into the area, approaching slowly and giving a wide distance between themselves and the dead man in the street.

Bart stared at the body and shook his head. "Didn't we just leave you with another body?"

"It is an unfortunate trend since we came to this town, Mister Hardwood." Slate spoke as softly as ever. "I'd like to think this might be the last of them."

Crowley stared at the dead man on the ground and shook his head. "At least this one seems willing to stay dead."

"That's a lovely thought." Slate removed his top hat for a moment and ran his fingers through the fine, pale hair on his head. "What now, Mister Crowley?"

"I'm ready to leave this place, Mister Slate."

"What about the witch?" It was one of the twins that spoke.

"I have taken away her fangs for another fortnight." Crowley looked at the woman and shrugged. "She dropped a dead man and hired the same man to kill your friend. I am sorry for your loss, but she is no longer my concern. Have the law take care of her or handle it yourselves."

She opened her mouth to speak again and then looked carefully at the expression on Crowley's face before nodding slowly.

The other sister looked at Slate and kept looking until he turned away, annoyed by the attention.

Within fifteen minutes Slate and Crowley had retrieved their horses from the stables. By then the sheriff was examining the dead man lying in the street.

"Will he come for us, Mister Crowley?"

"Doubtful. I am afraid I was impatient when I dealt with him last time. He might not be able to see us at all, Mister Slate."

"That could be a handy talent."

As if to prove his point one of the twins pointed directly at Crowley, and the sheriff looked his way, but seemed to see nothing.

"I've found it useful more than once, sir. There is a reason that I do not have stories told of me across all of Europe and the Orient, my good man."

"Indeed, sir."

Crowley looked at the twins. "Will you miss your lady friends?"

"I still find being ogled makes me uncomfortable, sir."

"You should work on your appearance then, Mister Slate."

"I've not much choice in how I look, Mister Crowley."

Crowley shook his head and a small smile played at his lips as he turned his horse to the west. "Perhaps. Perhaps not."

"Whatever do you mean?"

"Perception, Mister Slate. Even if you can't change the way you look, you might be able to change how you are perceived. We'll discuss that possibility, shall we?"

Slate said nothing for some time as he considered the implications of his companion's words. "Truly?"

"Perhaps, Mister Slate. For now, however, I prefer to move in silence for a time."

Slate nodded his head and said nothing as they rode away from the town. It was a comfortable silence, the sort that both of the men preferred.

THE TRICKSTER
OF PARADISE

R. B. WOOD

THADDEUS AND HIS Uncle Carl were working on the fence in the outer range when the sixteen-year-old's hairs stood on the back of his sweat-soaked neck.

The boy—young man—stood and looked over the land that had been in Thad's family for generations. He shielded his eyes from the blazing sun but couldn't see what had spooked him. The horses were grazing under the massive ash tree, tails occasionally flicking away flies. A light breeze made the grassland sway lazily to and fro.

"Look out!" barked Thad's uncle.

It was on the young man in the blink of an eye. A muscular form that had silently crept up on him. With a loud "Oooof!" Thad hit the ground hard while pushing the sinewy figure off him.

Laughter rose from the grasses.

His uncle, and a young man about Thad's age, were chuckling. The young man held out his hand. He was wearing tanned hides, moccasins, and one feather poking up from behind his head,

Blinking back tears of surprise and pain, Thad wanted nothing more than to punch the young Sioux right in his white teeth.

The young man caught his breath and grasped the outstretched arm. But as soon as they grasped hands, Thad pulled the other young man toward him. Off balance, both young men ended up in a tangled heap, each wrestling for the upper hand.

"Got ya!" said Thad, spitting out a bit of grass.

"Got you first," said the newcomer. After a moment of intense staring, both young men laughed and stood up, clapping each other on the back.

"That was good, White Feather," said Uncle Carl. "I didn't even hear you that time! I know my nephew is a bit dim sometimes . . . "

"Hey!" said Thad.

" . . . but he turned it around. What do I always say to you, young Thaddeus?"

"Tears are a waste. Get mad. Do something about how you feel . . . " intoned both Thad and White Feather together, rolling their eyes.

Turning to his best friend, Thad said, "What are you doing here? I thought you were going to be in town stocking up today?"

White Feather shrugged his shoulders. "We finished up early. And since all my chores were done early this morning, I stopped by your place. Your ma told me you were out here, and I thought I'd come out and scare the pants off you."

Thad snorted. "You didn't scare me!"

"Listen, you two, I have one more post to fix, then I'll be heading back home to get out of this heat. Why don't you two get out of here and kill each other somewhere else?"

The younger men's eyes lit up.

"The caves?" asked Thad.

"The caves!" confirmed White Feather.

"Thanks, Uncle!' shouted Thad as he and White Feather sprinted to the red rocks in the distance.

"Whoa, there!" called Uncle Carl. "Take your horse back to the stable! I ain't your hired hand, boy!"

"Will do!" said Thad, waving as he and White Feather changed course for his mare.

"You wanted to see me, general?"

The captain barely kept the sneer from creeping into his voice. The general was a small man with a gigantic salt and pepper mustache with an equally large belly to match. The younger man had no idea how this buffoon had gained his rank. All the captain knew was that he was glad he did. The better to make money out here at the expense of the army.

"Yes, captain, I damn well did!" The general pounded a pudgy hand onto his desk. "I've just heard some disturbing news, and I am surprised you didn't come to me first!"

The captain was a remarkable poker player. An unconcerned smile parted his lips. "What news are you referring to, sir."

'Well, captain, it seems there is a band of hooligans out and about in these parts harassing and thieving their way from here to Paradise!!" The old man's face flushed with emotion, and he gesticulated wildly. The captain caught a whiff of whiskey.

"Shocking, sir. It must be those Indians who live in the area."

"The damn heathens can't be allowed to rob innocents! We must bring law and order back to the area at once!"

"I'd take care of it, sir," The captain let his voice trail off deliberately. A plan was forming, and he let a concerned frown show on his face.

"I know that look, captain," spluttered the general. "Spit it out, man!"

He'd have to be careful. The old man was addle-minded, but he wasn't a complete idiot. A bit of verbal swordplay would be required. "Well, sir . . . the townsfolk of Paradise are pretty friendly with the natives . . . " began the captain as he paced thoughtfully. "wouldn't they take offense at us marching North to lock up those thieving animals?"

The general leaped up from his chair. "By God, you're right! The last thing we need is white folk rebelling out here, and we have enough problems with the redskins as it is."

The captain stopped his pacing and locked eyes with the general. "What do you suggest, sir?"

The senior officer waddled around his desk to stand before the captain. He stood a foot shorter than the younger man. "I suggest you handle it, captain. And don't come back until you've finished the job."

The captain saluted. "Right away, sir. I'll take my best men and sort out your little problem, and we'll be back from Paradise by nightfall."

The general patted the younger man on the arm. "Good, good. I knew you'd be able to sort this mess, captain. I wish I'd had a man like you at Bull Run. Dismissed."

Outside, the captain called to a filthy, unshaven man who had been mucking out the stables.

"Corporal," said the captain. "General's orders—get our men together and tell 'em to saddle up. We are finally gonna take out those damn heathens and the white traitors who befriended them. We leave within the hour."

The man wiped a bit of manure from his face. "Should we let our man in town know?"

"Yeah, drop him a telegram. Tell him it's finally time. And wipe the rest of that shit off yourself. You're a goddamn cavalryman!"

"We will be going to the deepest part of the caves today," intoned White Feather in a deep, foreboding voice. "But first, I must tell you a story. One handed down to us from our shaman—what you white-folk call a 'medicine man'."

Thad and his friend could see the great red rocks in the distance that housed the caves. They had to ride through Paradise to get there, but (God willing) if his ma didn't catch sight of him, they should be exploring in no time. White Feather's story, like his earlier ambush, would be meant to frighten him. No way he gets me again thought the young man.

"Go on. Tell me your medicine man's story."

"It was said that centuries ago," began White Feather in that fake basso voice he used when being dramatic. "The Ancient Ones told our old shaman that the bison was a sacred beast but that there was one such creature to be held in respect above the rest— the White Bison. It was said that such a rare and beautiful animal was the manifestation of the Ancient Ones themselves. This most sacred of creatures was not to be hunted, but treated as holy, as this White Bison was born on earth to guide us chosen people to live in harmony amongst all of nature."

"What does this have to do with the caves," blurted Thad, transfixed despite himself.

"I'm getting to that," replied White Feather, annoyed at the interruption. "But, unbeknownst to our ancestors, another beast had heard the story of the White Bison and became jealous. The beast was called Mica—the coyote trickster spirit. *Why,* thought the coyote, *was a freak to be given offerings and worship while the great Mica was chased away for stealing a single chicken?* So, the trickster formed a plan to fool the ancestors. He would transform into a bison himself, cover his shaggy fur in chalk from the nearby dry riverbed, then challenge the sacred White Bison to a duel and become the new favorite of the tribesmen!"

"If he could change into anything he wanted to," whispered Thad, "why didn't he just make himself white?"

"Shush," chided White Feather. "The jealous Mica carried out his plan and, at the full moon, presented himself atop the canyon and snorted a challenge to the White Bison. A great battle ensued, and the story was drawn and etched upon the walls of the sacred cave by the shaman of ancient times. The remainder of the ancient ones hid deep within the caves, frightened as two apparent bison gods fought for the world as they knew it.

Offerings and sacrifices were made. Songs were sung,

beseeching the gods for mercy. And still, the great battle raged in the canyon.

It is said that a whole night and day passed, and as a blood moon rose in the sky, the canyon fell into silence. The tribesmen made their way toward the cave's entrance, only to find the shaman dead and neither bison alive nor dead to be found. However, all the rocks in the canyon had turned the color of the blood moon and remained that color to this very day.

That, my dear friend, is what we will be going into the caves to see before the sun sets!"

The captain and his men rode to Paradise. The rogues, scoundrels, and murderers in his gang were hired and bought over time as his criminal enterprise had grown. Now that the general had heard of his crimes, he had convinced the racist blowhard that the peaceful Sioux tribe camped outside of Paradise had been to blame.

The fact that the old fat bastard had bought his lie that the townsfolk were involved was a bonus he never really expected to work.

His Dixie campaigns against the Rebs must have addled the old man's brains. So much the better.

The gang of riders crested a small rocky hill, and a dozen Sioux tipis were nestled together near a river surrounded by ash and fir trees. It was the quaint, picturesque tableau caught by a bleeding-heart painter back east.

Over the tops of the trees, the white wooden steeple of the lone church in Paradise could be seen, shimmering slightly in the afternoon heat.

The captain smiled and pulled a large wad of chewing tobacco out of a leather pouch.

He saw two small Indian children laughing and waving to him and his men.

"Isn't that the sweetest thing, boys," said the captain. His words led to guttural, hoarse laughter from his men. "They wanna say hello. So, let's show 'em how Americans say hello."

In unison, the men dug their spurs into their horses and rode toward the little village.

The gunfire and screaming started soon after.

It turned out that Thad's ma was chatting with the sheriff and a stranger dressed in black right in the middle of the main street of Paradise. Although he knew ma could smell when her son tried to dodge chores, he tried to coax his mare off the main thoroughfare. He felt White Feather attempting to shield himself—using Thad's body—from his mother's gaze.

Even Thad's mare trod slower.

"Thaddeus Eugene! You and your friend get yourself over here this instant!"

Most folks think of Thad as an adult. Sixteen was old enough to do most things nowadays. But when his ma spoke to him like that, the adult in him fled.

Without him guiding her, Thad's mare turned toward his ma. When you are a pastor preaching fire and brimstone from the pulpit, even the animals cower.

"You'll be explaining why you ain't with your uncle out mending the fence *later*," she said. "For now, I'd like you to meet Mr. Mortimer. He's in town for the day and was asking about Paradise."

"Hello," mumbled Thad.

"Nice to meet you, Mr. Mortimer," said White Feather, finally poking his head out from behind Thad.

"Well now," said the tall, gaunt-looking man in black. "It's nice to meet you both. You speak fine English, Mr. White Feather!"

How did he know White Feather's name, thought Thad.

"That would be my work," interjected Thad's ma proudly. "I taught him and my son together when they were just wee things. Thad's father, God rest his soul, had saved some of our Indian friends from some murderin' bandits way back when. Ever since, the local tribe and the townsfolk have gotten on mighty fine."

"It's a shame that most folks aren't that friendly to each other," said Mr. Mortimer. "This would be the kind of place where I'd settle down ~~in~~ if I were the settling type."

"And what do you do, Mr. Mortimer?" asked the Sherriff, a portly man with a bulbous red nose and a quick smile that made his massive mustache dance on his upper lip.

"Oh, I deal with the dead, mostly," he said. "Many places need my services these days."

Gunfire echoed in the distance. Terrified screams washed over the little town of Paradise.

"Jumpin' Josephat, What the hell . . . "

But the Sherriff never finished his sentence. A deputy who had been lurking near the conversation with the man in black had placed his revolver to the Sherriff's head.

"That would be the Injuns gettin' what they deserve, Sherriff. Time for some changes around here."

The deputy pulled the trigger.

The captain's men slaughtered the braves, women, and children. The scoundrels showed no mercy to the peaceful people who lived by the river. The tipis were torn down, and the bison hides used in their construction were collected by the captain's gang for resale later. Not one of the bandits was injured during the lightning assault.

In the distance, the church bells in Paradise began to ring. A warning to the surrounding townsfolk and any Indians who might have survived.

It was time to take the town.

"All right, boys. Our work is done here. Let the predators clean up the rest. Let's go raze us a town!"

The rabble cheered. The guttural, primal sounds were discordant with the desperate ring of church bells.

The blood-soaked earth of the ruined encampment might have disappeared, unknown in time. The silence following the massacre was finally broken by the sound of the wind. Black grains of sand swirled in a circle, and a crescendo of an unearthly, mournful wail added a strange coda to this scene of death and suffering.

Mr. Mortimer appeared from the twisting black sand, and a black horse attached to an equally black steed appeared with him.

He knelt in reverence and respect for the people whose blood seeped into the parched ground.

"I would have gladly settled here," he muttered. But there is always too much work to do."

The Trickster of Paradise

The sun's heat bore down on Thad as his feet kicked up crimson dust. It rose in the air, choking him, and he nearly coughed. *If I cough, I'm dead,* he thought. His heart hammered at his ribcage, sounding like the tribal drums he sometimes heard echoing around the red rock canyon. His friend, White Feather, could run silently. Thad hoped he had learned enough to do the same. *They saw him. They were coming.*

Thad's mother would have called them "signs sent by the God" in one of her sermons. After what he had seen, Thad was convinced that God didn't exist; no benevolent God would let good people die like that.

Paradise was a young town—Thad had been the first baby born there. In the beginning, when old man Whipple and his wife opened their saloon back in 1871, there had been some trouble with the "locals." But the incident that had taken the life of Thad's pappy had changed all that. Now his family and the townsfolk of Paradise lived in harmony with those whose land had been stolen. His ma practiced the love and tolerance she preached.

She practiced the fire and brimstone stuff too. Thad's best friend knew that.

White Feather.

He was dead now. Thad fought back the burning tears and the bloody memory that threatened to overwhelm him.

The town of Paradise felt like its name, at least that's what ma always proclaimed. As a woman of God—a genuine believer, unlike most folk, she was truly happy in Paradise. Thad didn't take too kindly to some of the things in the Good Book, but he was happy in Paradise too.

Thad's ma—one of only a few women preachers back then— had said that the natives were holy people that deserved respect. That was at his pappy's funeral, and it had been right after that when he and White Feather had become friends. Those were the happiest days of his life.

And God took all that from him. God and those thieving som'bitches.

Thad wondered if these spinning thoughts were a prelude to his own death.

The sheriff was killed first. Shot in the head by a traitor. One of the deputies had got it into his head that more money could be made switching sides.

Thad's chest spasmed, and he covered his mouth. He was fighting a losing battle with his young body as he struggled to remain quiet. He was sure a cough or a sob wanted to escape from his cracked lips.

His chest heaved again, and a cough echoed mockingly around the canyon walls.

A curse was thrown in his direction. Thad looked over his shoulder and could see the dust from the bandit's running footsteps. They were closer now.

Run like you're on a cloud, Thad. Real quiet-like. That's what White Feather always said.

A lump rose in his throat at the thought of White Feather's words. He remembered how they started shooting everyone in town. Men, women, children—it didn't matter to these monsters. White Feather took a shotgun blast to the face. Thad could still smell the coppery bits of brain matter that clung to his clothes.

The soulless bastards came for those who took refuge in the church next.

Before the telegraph office had been lit on fire, a message had been sent to Cheyenne begging for help from the army. Thad's ma had said so to try and reassure the folk huddled in the Sanctuary. No one knew if the message had been received or not. No one knew how long it would take for the military to arrive to help, even if they got the message. Troubles with other tribes and the Mexicans were the priority for the army, while a small town being overrun with criminals was far down the list of priorities. Caught in the middle— as was always the case in such things—were the hard-working townsfolk, ranches, and God-fearing Christians of the region. It was the blood of the innocent that turned the ground crimson during the dark times.

Thad thought about one of Ma's recent sermons where she had called the troublemakers "heathens" and "devils." The small congregation led by Thad's mother would not be immune from reprisals, as his ma had preached fire and brimstone in the bandit's direction. The peace-loving culture nurtured by ma was the exact opposite of the hellion bandits.

Ma was trying to keep everyone's spirits up with talk of the army and other comforting thoughts when the bandits had blasted their way into the church. That's when she'd told Thad to run.

Thad should have helped more with the frightened townsfolk,

and he should have helped his ma more. But the image of White Feather's faceless body had been all the young man could see in his mind.

Paradise had gone from peace to war in the blink of an eye. Thad went from learning to run quiet-like to running for his life from violent men with knives and guns.

"We's gonna git ya, little mouse!" called one of Thad's pursuers. He had to focus, to breathe. His mother had taught him that. Fear is nothing but a weak thought; walk through it, and it will disappear.

Was ma even alive?

He was thirsty. He needed water, but Thad closed his eyes and focused on breathing. The water didn't matter. The heat didn't matter. The scrapes he'd gotten during his escape didn't matter. His sore feet didn't matter. When he opened his eyes, he was calmer. His brain began to work again when he noticed the caves. The caves! He used to play here with White Feather all the time! He set off again, faster this time. Thad launched himself toward the forbidding yet familiar entrance with renewed strength and determination. Instinct had brought him here.

White Feather had told him the story of these caves. But since everybody in Paradise knew the legend—even a young white man knew the tale that surrounded all the ancient Indian holy places in the area. He and his friend had explored many of them, which is why, when his ma told him to run, he ran straight to the holy caves with the carvings. Even the bandits were aware of this place's sacred nature and reverence and might think twice before following Thad inside.

The battle had been captured upon the cave walls where Thad had come to hide. But there was a curious coda to the story. Depicted on the walls were two white bison—one with a mouth dripping with blood—and no one knew which petroglyph was the sacred bison and which was the trickster. And it was said during each moonrise that the cave drawings would continue the fight anew—a never-ending contest for dominance.

Yes, Thad knew the story well. A different version of the story was told to the town's white children by their parents to keep them in their beds and away from the dangerous, crumbling ruins of the caves. The young Thad hoped that the bandits were told the white version of the story and that they would see the faded drawings of the bison at the entrance. It may not stop them, but it might give the criminals pause before following him into the ancient holy grounds, allowing Thad to hide within the dark labyrinth.

The young man swiftly made his way over the dusty, familiar ground, through the gaping maw embedded in the red rocks, and into the cave's heart. With a typical young man's careless abandon, he and White Feather had thoroughly explored the upper levels of these interconnected caves—the tale of the white bison only heightened their excitement and sense of adventure.

But the lower levels had frightened the young men.

While he loved the story of the White Bison, he had never really believed the legend was true. Not once in all his and his friend's explorations had they seen a hint of battling bison etchings or the image of a bison with blood dripping from a fanged mouth.

Thad stopped short. He was now deep inside the caves. The darkness enveloped Thad and threatened to swallow him. He'd never gone further than the light before, and his body shivered with renewed fear. Suddenly, a white light shone. It wasn't the sort of light from either the sun or a lamp but the brightest white light he had ever seen. He covered his eyes; fear and curiosity engaged in a battle for his young mind. He traveled further into the cave and then saw—yes! On the wall was an ancient etching of a white bison! Its faded red eyes looked out at the young man, almost mockingly. From its mouth, rivulets of brownish-red oozed down the stone. There was a clatter of metal on rock. Distracted, Thad turned from the wall. When he turned back, the faded bison carving with dripping blood was gone. Darkness and fear enveloped him once more.

There was another clatter and a curse. Thad's hopes for a reprieve from the hunting bandits were dashed. They had followed him into the caves.

"Light a goddamn match, you useless shit. The captain will hang us by our balls if we lose him."

A harsh hiss of a curse followed another barrage of cursing. Thad tried to fade into the shadows.

"We are coming for you, little mouse," called the same man, his voice echoing off the dry, dusty cave walls. "No buffalo legend can save your ass from your fate." The bandit's companion laughed, and it was a horrible, mirthless sound.

"There. Old torches. That little bastard won't get away now!"

Careful to scrape away his dusty footprints, Thad moved further into the cave, realizing only now that his gambit had one major flaw. There was no longer any way he could get past the two thugs and escape through the only way out. The legend of the magical white bison hadn't even slowed the men down—of course, it hadn't. If they were willing to storm God's house, a mere Indian folktale wouldn't stop them. His only option now was to hide, and his stupid boyish plan might get him killed after all. One chance—he knew these caves better than his hunters, and even thru the dim gloom of the sunlight-deprived spaces, he could make his way quietly.

Quickly. Follow me!

The voice was like a gentle breeze on his ear. The scent of the plains and the musk of a large animal filled his nostrils. Thad's heart skipped a beat. The legend was true! It had to be! The young man was sure that the white bison was no mere story but fact. And it was here with him now. His brain spun with possibilities that a mighty presence could provide. For all his mother's teachings of God and the Son of Man, he had never actually *believed* before.

Follow me, boy.

Thad outpaced his pursuers, turning left down one rocky passage, right down another. Through his guardian, Thad instinctively knew which paths led to cave-ins, covered in sharp stones that would slice through his boots, and which direction would allow him to move quickest. The best hiding spots, whispered the bison, were lower into the pitch blackness. Cold, damp air washed over the young man, and his sweat-soaked clothes made him shiver as goose flesh rippled over his arms, legs, and back.

Down he went, following the quiet voice and the brief flashes of white light until he found himself in a massive chamber which glittered with a strange, jewel-like quality. On the wall opposite from where Thad had entered was an enormous series of etchings he had never seen before.

For all their bravado, he and White Feather had never had enough courage to follow the caves to this point. His friend would have loved to see these petroglyphs! The guardian showed its white light on the wall, the light itself shrinking until it focused on one of the cave pictures. A beautiful white bison with red eyes with droplets oozing from its mouth looked down at the young man.

The etching smiled, showing—not the flat teeth of an herbivore but a predator's sharp fangs. Thad's heart filled with joy, for if this drawn creature was real, its role as a guardian *must* be real too. Thad was sure it was the same bison he had seen earlier, the one revered in all the old native stories White Feather had told him. He recognized the brilliant beams of white light radiating all around the creature and the animalistic smile. The faded red eyes were focused on him.

He felt a sense of warmth that reminded him of his mother's touch, smelled the scent of freshly baked cake that she would leave cooling for her Bible study group, and heard the sound of the sweet songs she sang at night when Thad had trouble sleeping. All were rolled into this carved image of a glowing, smiling bison.

They come.

The bandits were coming closer. He either had to hide or take a chance that this creature was the guardian he needed.

Hiding isn't a real man's choice.

Thad took a chance on a legend.

"Great Bison," the young man panted, trying to calm both his breathing and pounding heart, "If you truly be real, as in the old stories, I need your help."

"I am here. I am real. I will gladly help you, boy, but what is in it for me?" rasped the bison.

The voice came from everywhere and nowhere at once. Thad was so startled by the sound, like two rocks grinding together, that he tripped over his own feet, landing with a thud and a gasp of pain.

"Wha . . . what?" asked Thad in a harsh whisper. His hands reflexively grabbed at his chest. He must have landed on a rock, cracking a rib.

"You said a prayer to the Great Bison, so I decided to answer you," said the etching, shrugging its shaggy shoulders.

Even as Thad watched, the old, faded image of a bison moved. It shook its massive head, then snorted and pawed at the rocks. Finally, it yawned, then looked down at the young man once more with its glowing red eyes.

"It's true, then. The story about you is true!" Thad couldn't help it. The words slipped out as pain wrapped around his chest.

The bison began to nuzzle the rocks as if searching for a delectable piece of grass. It continued this way for what seemed to

Thad an eternity. Finally, it looked back at the child. "They still tell my story after all this time. That pleases me. What is your name, boy?"

"Tha-Thaddeus," he said through gritted teeth. He realized he was still sitting in the dirt and scrambled to rise to a position of supplication, as was proper. After all, it wasn't every day you met a legend.

Thad moved too quickly, and his rib throbbed. He let out a small groan that echoed off the chamber's walls.

"Slow down, boy. You have already injured yourself. Allow me to fix that." The bison's eyes glowed even brighter for a moment. "There. Is that better?"

"I," began Thad and then stopped. The pain from his cracked ribs had mysteriously vanished. His breathing slowed, and even his sore feet and the scrapes he'd gotten from the sharp rocks outside the cave disappeared. His parched throat no longer felt like an old piece of jerky.

He felt both watered and fed. He hadn't even realized he'd been hungry until the pangs had been satisfied.

"Yes, much better, thank you!" Thad averted his eyes from the bison.

"Now. I have been watching you for some time, young one, and it appears you have a little problem with a few bandits. Would that be correct, Mr. Thaddeus?"

Thad bowed his head further.

"Well, I will, of course, protect you if that is your true wish," said the bison. "But I must ask for something in return."

Thad looked up at the colorful etching, frowning, as his curiosity overrode his training and said, "You protected that Indian tribe in the story without a return favor." Thad, eyes widening at his own boldness, hastily averted his gaze again.

"Boy, the protection of my tribe was paid for many times over by the songs and tribute my people provided. You, as of yet, have not earned my favor, and all blessings must be paid for."

A noise sounded up the corridor. Thad glanced back.

"Yes, little one," said the rock-carved bison. "The hunters come for their prey. What shall it be?"

"What do you want?" asked Thad sharply. His heart was now pounding so hard he thought it would burst from his chest. He was desperate to escape the damn bandits who invaded his town. So desperate that he was willing to make a deal with a magical talking bison.

The white bison's smile widened. It licked its lips.

"What do I want? Dear boy, I want to be free of this rotting cave! To see the sun, to taste the grass! What does every living creature want? To live free!"

"How do I do that? How do I get you out of this cave? You are carved into the solid rock!"

Muffled voices echoed around Thad. The bandits drew close.

"There is a stone near where you kneel, young one. That will do. Just hold it to the wall close to me and say these words: 'I remove you from this cave to this stone by my own free will!'"

Thad was confused. The rock by his knees was just a plain old stone. Like any other lying in the cave. Was this stone somehow special? Like the cup Christ touched at the Last Supper? Or the nails of the Cross that had pierced the Lord's flesh? Was this stone touched by faith—his faith? Was his act of reverence to this magical being unique in some way?

Scrape. Laughter. "Where are you, little mouse?" They were close.

With no choice that he could see, Thad grabbed the stone and approached the glowing carving on the wall. Too much blood had been spilled in the town already. The sheriff. White Feather. The image of his friend, bloodied and faceless, lying like discarded trash in the dusty street. Too many others were shot with lead or stabbed by steel. Thad had to do *something* to defeat the cursed bandits. "Agreed, White Bison," he said. Then, putting some of his own steel into his voice, he recited the oath, "I remove you from this cave to this stone by my own free will!"

The bison shrunk in size and stepped, tentatively at first, onto the rock in Thad's hand. Thad did not know if the bison had heard his verbal subterfuge. He had just finished stuffing the stone with the etched creature out of sight when two bandits burst around the corner with torches held high, six-shooters drawn.

"Got you, little mouse!" shouted the lead thug triumphantly.

Under the blazing sun, the criminals frog-marched Thad back to Paradise. Many of the buildings were smoldering from fires set by the marauding bandits. He was led to his ma's church—the only building still intact. Thad saw two more bandits with Winchesters standing outside the double doors, and another was in the bell tower steeple with a telescope of some kind.

He was unceremoniously shoved through the doors and muttered a silent prayer as he stumbled into the central Sanctuary.

Thad was manhandled toward the altar, where he found not only his family but also a dozen of the townsfolk, all bloody and filthy from being dragged from their homes through the streets and ranches in the middle of the day. What struck Thad first was the smell. Typically, this sacred space would be ripe with fragrant offerings—flowers picked from his mother's garden or gifted by a thankful parishioner. Now, the stench of blood, sweat, and worse assaulted Thad's nostrils. Below a wood carving of the Crucifixion, the prisoners had their hands tied behind their backs and were sitting in a circle, some in their own filth.

"Thaddeus!" called his uncle. He attempted to hug the young man and nearly toppled over as he stood. He ended up falling over onto Mrs. Greenlaw and Jasper Fallow—the butcher's young son. His cheeks were streaked with tears, and it broke Thad's heart to see his uncle normally so stoic, so distraught. They locked eyes for perhaps a second or two, then one of the bandits clubbed his uncle with the butt of his pistol. His uncle took the blow, staggered, and glared at his captor. The bandit smacked his uncle with the back of his hand, sending the man to his back, blood flowing from his nose and a cut on his lip. Thad looked up at the wooden Jesus.

*Why won't you do something? Why won't you do **anything**?*

Before anyone could react, the invaders had their guns drawn and aimed at the townsfolk.

No words were spoken, and none were needed. Only the soft sobs of Thad's uncle broke the furious silence.

"I'm sorry they caught you, Thaddeus."

A tall, commanding figure of a woman, her hair prematurely greying, called over to Thad. She, too, was bound with hands tied at her back. It was the preacher—his mother.

"Ma!" the young man cried and threw his arms around her.

"I love you," she said, leaning her head onto her son's.

One of the bandits pulled mother and son apart.

Angry muttering from the captured townsfolk began to rise,

and their captors took a step toward them, the sound of cocking Colts silencing any potential trouble.

The standoff was broken when the former deputy entered, making his way to the group.

"None of that, you rabble. You already have enough graves to dig today. You," he said, pointing at the bandit who had hit Thad's uncle, "The captain wants to see you. The rest of you men stay here and guard these injun-lovers."

A moment later, the double doors to the church banged closed. A loud click confirmed they were locked in.

Giving Thad a reassuring smile, the young man's mother turned and knelt by her still bleeding brother.

"Carl," she whispered, gazing at her sibling fondly but shaking her head. "You were always as thick as a stump. Thaddeus, since these heathens haven't seen fit to tie you up, please, could you come help clean up your uncle?"

Thad let out a soft noise, something between a sob and a frustrated cry, and rushed over to his fallen uncle. The big man slumped to the ground, and Thad, after a moment of searching, found a cloth on the altar. He wiped the blood from his uncle's nose and mouth. The day had caught up to the young man like an iron horse trying to make up time on the rails to Albuquerque. Thad's vision blurred, and his nose ran while a guttural sob escaped his lips.

"Hush, young one. I'm fine," said Thad's uncle softly. And to prove his point, he smiled. His two front teeth were missing.

"Rest, my brother," said Thad's mother, her voice commanding yet compassionate.

All at once, angry whispers began again. Thad moved to listen. *A plan*, he thought. *They needed a plan, and his mother was the most intelligent and wisest person in the town.*

" . . . all that is left of my shop," hissed the blacksmith.

" . . . my entire family, dead!" wailed another.

" . . . too strong . . . " muttered a third.

Thad's mother gave a low hiss. The townsfolk fell silent at once.

"I shall speak with this captain the bandits have spoken about. Perhaps there is some way to save what remains."

A cacophony burst forth as the prisoners raised their voices.

Mother could not be talking about surrendering to these invaders, thought Thad furiously. *We must fight!*

The pastor shook her head. "I must try. Some of the scoundrels are God-fearing men. I heard them complaining about desecrating our church. Perhaps if we appeal to the more religious of these bandits, we could sow seeds of discord among them."

"Where is the army?" spat one of the ranchers. "We sent them a distress telegram! They must have gotten the message! The fort is only a few hours away. Surely help should arrive soon . . . ."

"The army is *in* on it," snarled the butcher's son, Jasper. Didn't you hear that piece of dung say something about 'The captain?' We are all alone out here!"

"Silence." When Thad's mother spoke in that strong, whispered tone of hers, even the cows listened.

"I have decided," she said. "There will be no more discussion. We must take care of our injured and prepare for whatever may come next. I will reach out to—"

At that moment, there was a loud metallic click, and the doors to the Sanctuary slammed open. A group of bandits marched in and positioned themselves around the prisoners. A second later, a man of average height in a blue army uniform, complete with a calvary saber attached to his side, walked into the room. He wrinkled his nose at the smell and turned his beetle-like eyes toward the townsfolk. There was a sense of power emanating from the man and a sense of cruelty as well. Everyone in the room shrank away from him.

Everyone except Thad's mother.

"Who speaks for the people of this town?" barked the soldier.

"Since your men have seen fit to slaughter the mayor, I do," rumbled Thad's ma. She met the captain's gaze calmly, without challenge, but without flinching. Thad had never been prouder of his mother than at that moment.

"Ah," said the captain sounding almost bored. "A woman preacher. Don't that beat all, boys?"

Cruel laughter permeated the circle of prisoners.

"I shall speak slow and plainly, then, shall I?" chuckled the captain.

Thad wanted to kick the man for his lack of respect and wipe the self-righteous smirk off the soldier's face.

"We have conquered your town as well as the surrounding ranches. All this region's industry, farms, animals, and resources are now ours, down to the last chicken. You all can work for us and live or die in your paltry little church. That choice is only for those who serve a purpose, anyway." The captain sneered at Thad's mother, "Oh, don't worry, preacher. you are still young enough to have a new purpose for my men."

More laughter from the gun-wielding bandits echoed around them.

Thad's uncle stood slowly and took his place by his sister's side.

"I don't give a rat's ass who you think you are, *captain*," he said, spitting blood at the soldier. All I know is that you are a damn thief and a weakling. Your desecration of my sister's church speaks of the ungodliness of your actions this day."

It happened so fast; Thad had no time to look away. All he saw was the gleam of a blade, a whoosh of sound, and a soft thump as his uncle's head fell heavily to the ground. The man's body stood headless for a moment, then, blood gushing from the stump of his neck, slumped toward Thad. His uncle's heart spent its last few beats splashing crimson over his nephew. The young man watched with horror as his uncle's bloody head rolled to a stop next to the altar, eyes blinking and mouth moving wordlessly. His uncle's eyes locked onto Thad just as the light faded from them. In mere seconds, his uncle was gone.

"Any other people of 'good moral character' wishing to say their piece?" asked the captain calmly. He nodded, as the only responses to his question were impotent, furious gazes and shocked silence.

"Good. Then it is settled. Now, untie these walking dung heaps so they can clean up this mess. These hog-fuckers know what'll happen if they try anything else stupid." The captain turned on his heels and left, wiping the blood from his saber with a white handkerchief as he went.

The shadows seemed to follow him out of the Sanctuary as the doors closed behind him.

Much later that evening, after the body of Thad's uncle had been cleaned as well as possible and laid with respect near the heart of the altar, the young Thad found himself alone in the darkest corner of the church. Thad had heard too many words of condolences, had seen too many tears, and needed to be as alone as one could get, trapped in a small church filled with hand-wringing adults. His ma was compassionate and took her time to speak to everyone in turn. She loved people, and she loved helping them see the "wonders that were Jesus." That is probably why a woman with her strengths became a respected preacher. Thad was fine with one person, maybe two, if he knew them well. But the stress of the day and the packed crowd of townsfolk that all wanted to tell him how sorry they were or what a wonderful man his uncle had been. It was all too much. He was overwhelmed.

Besides, he wanted to be angry and alone.

Ma had once said that an angry man never made good decisions and that his anger needed to be tempered, like the Lord. But Thad was more like Jesus when he overturned the money lender's tables in the temple court. That Jesus, Thad understood. Out of respect for his ma and the church, he avoided taking his anger out on anyone, especially her. Using a mother's intuition or a preacher's experience, she must have known what he was feeling and kept her distance. She spent time speaking to her flock and praying over her brother's body. Men and women both let tears of sorrow and frustration roll silently down their faces, mourning for Carl and others that still lay in the streets of Paradise. Thad observed them from the long purple shadows. He was glad for the silence, for he wanted to lose himself in his seething thoughts and tears.

Thad heard the wisdom of his uncle's words "Tears are a waste. Get mad. *Do* something about how you feel. Just don't tell your ma I told you that, okay?"

He was gonna live those words in memory of his uncle. Thad's temper would rule his heart now. *How dare those heathens come into their town? How dare they desecrate his mother's church? How dare they kill his uncle?*

He clenched his fists and began to shake. He felt helpless, like a beetle caught under foot or a blade of grass in the mouth of...

Do something about how you feel.

. . . the mouth of a bison.

He reached into his pocket and felt around. The stone was still there.

"Terrible," whispered a low, gravelly voice. "That was your uncle, was it not, boy?"

Thad blinked, startled, as he had all but forgotten the bison still on the stone hidden in his pocket. He looked around quickly, but no one seemed to have heard.

No one was watching.

He removed the stone from his pocket and found the glowing beast lounging lazily as if enjoying the sunshine on a grassy plain. He used both hands to shield the white glow from the rest of his cellmates.

"Can you turn off your light?" asked Thad.

"Oh, of course, little one," drawled the etching. "It is such a small favor that I shall do it for free out of respect for your uncle.

The glow from the stone went out. Only the beast's red eyes glimmered in the dark. Thad looked over his shoulder, but no one seemed to notice.

"Is that more to your liking, young one?"

"I thought you'd protect me," hissed Thad. He looked around again, but still, no one was paying any attention.

"And so, I did!" huffed the miniature bison sounding offended. "That soldier was going to execute *you* for your uncle's insolence and because of your escape attempt. I made him change his mind at the last second."

"What?!" shouted Thad. Now people began to stare. Even his mourning mother turned to look at him, one eyebrow raised. He could see tear streaks under her eyes, reflected by the fires outside that were still burning in Paradise. Thad bowed his head in apology and waited for his audience to turn back to their own business. When the young man was sure no one was paying him any attention, he moved toward one of the stained-glass windows where he could see remaining fires. The saloon was gone, as was the bank. The jail and general store still burned, the flames dancing across the dried timbers creating mocking shadows that twisted across the pews and prisoners alike. The burning building matched the heat of Thad's anger, and he held the stone closer to his face.

The bison's eyes twinkled.

"You killed my uncle," Thad whispered to the etched figure. The bison held the young man's furious gaze for a moment, then snorted and shook its tail at a curious fly that had wandered too close to its stone.

"Our deal was," said the bison smugly. "You get me out of that cave, and I would protect you, was it not? You said nothing about protecting anyone else. I have upheld my part of the bargain. Now let me off this stone. I am already bored with my lack of roaming space."

At those infuriating words, a new plan formed in Thad's mind. He wasn't helpless against the bandits after all—far from it. Thad had a most mighty potential ally. But he had already lost one verbal sparring match with the cursed carving that cost his uncle's life. Legends told of hapless mortals who engaged verbally with the spirits and other higher beings. The Greek plays his ma made him read were full of wordplay and taunts called stichomythia. This whole nightmare was becoming Thad's own Greek tragedy. Although he doubted anyone would sing songs or write poems about him anytime soon. The young man's following words would be critical to his plan for revenge.

"I removed you from the cave, little beast," Thad whispered through clenched teeth. "I said nothing about letting you off this rock. I believe I know of a new home for you—seeing as we will be digging many graves soon." He pretended to slip the stone back into his pocket.

The bison leaped up, dislodging bits of red stone dust. Thad could not be sure, but he thought he saw a look of panic in the creature's massive brown eyes.

"Ah! Well done, young one. It is true, then. We have both met the words, if not the spirit of our original agreement." The bison's glowing red eyes narrowed. "Shall we enter into another bargain then? Your lot does not seem to have improved since we first met."

"What do you have in mind?" asked Thad. His mind raced, forming the sentences as carefully as he had learned his numbers and words from his mother's schooling. He wished desperately for his uncle's council, as word puzzles and poker were his favorite games to play and would be more beneficial to him than long-dead poets. At the thought of his uncle, a sudden pang of sadness threatened to overwhelm Thad, and the emotion had to be quickly shoved aside to be dealt with later.

The bison paced across the stone. "I can get you out of here, to be sure. I can make you invisible so that none could see you in the darkness, and then you could get us far away from this place—to the mountains or the sea if you wish. All before those bandits notice you are gone. In return, I ask for my complete freedom. From this stone. From the cave. From any vessel that could be a prison."

"Hmm," said Thad, rubbing his chin thoughtfully. "We still have a problem, great White Bison. You get everything you want in the deal you suggest, but I am dealt a losing hand."

The bison snorted impatiently. "It is a fair deal, boy."

"No, it isn't. See, I want all of us to be free. Me, my family, the people of Paradise, and any others these scoundrels have not yet killed. Then, and only then, will you be granted your wish. That is *my* price for your freedom. We all get to roam free and smell the grasslands, as you put it. Or none of us do. It is your choice, but I remind you that your alternative is to spend the rest of eternity in a grave next to a rotting corpse."

Thad held his breath.

"You are rather wise for one so young," said the etching, bowing its head in defeat. "What you ask for is potent magic indeed."

Thad shrugged his shoulders and played his last hand, a bluff. He started to return the stone to his pocket.

"Wait! I never said I could not grant you your desire. I only said it would take powerful magic!"

Thad brought the stone to eye level.

"I am only a carving of a bison," said the creature, eyes glowing brightly once more. "Full freedom for so many would require . . . a body of my own. A truly living creature."

"There are plenty of living creatures in and about Paradise. You can have whomever you like," said Thad.

"Whomever I like? Maybe," said the bison, one hoof digging at its stone absently, as if in deep thought.

"I'm curious, guardian. What will happen?" began Thad, licking his lips, "if I bury this stone with my uncle and you are still a prisoner on it?"

Bison looked annoyed. "I would return to the cave where my creator had used chisel, blood, and sweat to make me."

"So, no eternal grave, but back to the caves. Caves, I will take great pleasure in dynamiting closed forever. It would be as if you were buried then. Or help us all. I believe I have articulated a mutually beneficial bargain and a clear choice for you. Would you not agree, bison?"

"Hmm," replied the beast. "I will need more than your word on this, young one. I will need a drop of your blood to seal our bargain and to make this magic work."

"Do we have an agreement?" Thad moved the stone fractionally closer to his pocket.

"We do," growled the bison.

Thad looked around, his eyes falling on a bit of broken glass near his feet. He bent, picked up the shard, and cut his thumb. He smeared a drop of blood on the stone. The bison immediately sprang toward the blood and lapped at the stain until nothing more than a red smear remained on its carved, fanged mouth.

"Done and done," said the White Bison. "Tomorrow, the captain and his men plan on moving the survivors of this town to the army fort, where you will be put to work or death. You must tell everyone here to be ready tonight."

"For what? And how do I make them believe a young man like me?" hissed Thad.

"Such a clever young man as yourself should have no trouble at all convincing them. Start with your mother; she will help you convince the rest," the bison whispered. "Show her my rock, and she will believe and convince the others your word is true.

The preacher listened to Thad's story. Growing up, Thad knew that the one thing ~~she~~ his ma hated more than sin and more than the Devil himself, was lying. Pappy used to lie to ma all the time, and she always caught him at it. It broke her heart, and Thad had promised never to lie to his mother.

So, he told her the whole story, beginning with White Feather's death, the chase to the cave, and the encounter with the white bison petroglyph. Almost all of it.

Then he showed her the rock. The bison played its role well, snorting and galloping across the stone.

He left out the bit about the second bargain. Ma hated gambling almost as much as lying.

After all, he thought. *Lies of omission aren't really lies, are they?*

To the preacher's credit, she listened to her son tell his story in rapid, hushed whispers. When he finished, she only asked a few questions, and once Thad had answered, she nodded and called the remaining prisoners together.

The bison bit Thad's hand as the young man nervously fingered the stone in his pocket.

"What?" he hissed.

"You should rest. That way, you will be better prepared for tomorrow morning."

"No," said Thad. "I want to fight. I want to help."

The guardian chuckled once more. "You have already helped, young one. Sleep now. Tomorrow, all will be crystal clear!"

A massive yawn escaped from Thad. His body felt heavy, so very heavy. *What is happening?* He thought in a panic. *Ma.* But he couldn't make his mouth form the word.

Thad's legs wobbled underneath him. It was a struggle for him to walk. He had to get to his mother. But wait, why was he walking anyway. The darkness in the Sanctuary seemed to swirl around Thad. His vision blurred, and he fell to the church's wooden floor. He was asleep before any more thoughts could form.

The stone with the etching fell from Thad's hand and bounced on the floor. The small rock glowed bright white for the briefest moment, and the light extinguished.

"Sleep, young one, and prepare for something wonderful," chuckled the White Bison.

Paradise had been sacked completely. The thieves had grabbed anything not nailed down. Bloated bodies remained in the street, and the flies and buzzards had begun their work. Night had fallen, and a crescent moon along with the stars witnessed as coyotes and other night scavengers circled the broken and smoldering embers of Paradise, looking for a chance at a meal.

The captain was furious. Instead of setting the prisoners to work digging graves, the men had looted the saloon and had drunk most of the liquor he was under orders to bring back to the fort. The former deputy, however, in a moment of brilliant evil, had suggested they bring the Sioux dead from the local encampment they had raided earlier into the town to make it look as if the savages had attacked Paradise.

"This undertaker named Mortimer I met in town before the fun started, gave me the idea. He said he'd be able to clean up the bodies when it was all over. Said he'd do it for nothing, the jackass. He wanted to wait 'til we were all done here. It's a perfect solution," slurred the deputy, clutching a bottle of whiskey, his breath smelling like death itself. "The town will be labeled heroes who died for the country. The government will send us more men and supplies to avenge the deaths of these poor assholes, and we will be able to retire surrounded by buxom whores."

The captain had been tempted to remove this man's head when he discovered the state of the scum he brought to his cause, but his plan made sense. So, he let the drunken fool live.

Besides, he'd make a perfect scapegoat down the line, should the captain need one.

A future Senator, maybe president, always needed scapegoats.

He enjoyed a five-dollar cigar stolen from the late mayor's stores. With a smirk, he was on his way back to the church to see how far that preacher lady would go to protect her son.

An unearthly bright white light caught his attention through the haze of smoke clinging to Paradise like a burial shroud.

"What the hell is that?" he muttered, squinting his eyes. If it were the general and those damn Buffalo Soldiers of the hundred and twenty-fifth, he'd be in trouble, and he'd have to use his scapegoat earlier than anticipated.

More white lights appeared. The wind switched direction, and the soldier got a clearer look. It wasn't a light at all. It was an animal. A white buffalo stood on the crest overlooking the city.

"I'll be damned," said the captain. "That will make one helluva trophy on my wall. Gotta go get my rifle."

Just then, another bright light appeared. And a third. A half dozen. A score. More now than the captain could count. These new apparitions—for that's what the soldier thought they were—seemed to be larger animals. Horses.

Horses with riders. Riders wearing bright, glowing war paint.

"Mary, mother of God!" the captain exclaimed. Savages. It was some savage trick. "Indians!" he shouted. "You drunk fuckers get up. We are under attack!"

The illuminated spectral spirits of the Sioux let out a bloodcurdling war cry and moved as one toward what was left of the town. The shades were led by the lone white buffalo.

The beast had glowing red eyes.

The men the captain tried to rally were cruel and bloodthirsty but drunk and undisciplined. The spectral warriors roared into town with ghostly axes held high and phantom bows at the ready.

The warriors themselves all had various shimmering wounds that leaked a silvery liquid.

How in God's name do you kill something you've already killed, thought the captain in a moment of panicked realization. The men staggered out of tents and the remains of buildings, only to be cut down by the vengeful spirits. Bullets did not affect the ghouls, but the weapons of the ghostly warriors struck home again and again. Limbs and heads were separated from bodies, and the gunfire that had exploded from the frightened men faltered, finally stopping moments later.

The captain, a coward at heart as most murderers were, had hid, watching for a chance to escape the slaughter. While the ghostly horde hunted his men in every part of Paradise, he noticed that the church itself was left untouched by the wave of death that had rolled through the town.

He made his way past freshly spilled blood and offal, shaking with every step he took. He had almost made it to the church steps when a tall, thin man—a flesh and blood man dressed all in black— suddenly appeared between him and the double doors that lead to the Sanctuary.

"Evening, captain," he said, tipping his hat as if this was a casual encounter in a general store. "Name's Mortimer."

The captain drew his saber. "I don't give a fucking whore's twat who you are. Get out of my way, or I will slice you in twain."

The man in black clicked his tongue. "Now, captain is that any way to meet your maker. I told that deputy I'd be cleaning up as soon as your little adventure was done. I am, if nothing else, a man of my word."

The captain lunged at the man in black but never made it further than the first step. A glowing white buffalo knocked the soldier out of his boots and impaled him on its horns. It tossed the body into the air with a flick of its massive, shaggy head, and the broken soldier landed in a heap against the side of the church.

The White Bison and Mortimer eyed each other for a moment, then the big animal snorted once and turned away, its glowing fur turning to dust as it moved into the night.

Mortimer turned and knelt by the dead captain.

"Nobody will ever know your name," said Mortimer. "Now, my work is done," he said.

With those words, the man in black and all those murdered in

Paradise, the Sioux encampment, and surrounding ranches vanished in a swirl of black dust. Silence returned to the canyon

Thad woke with a start to the whispered, fearful voices of the townsfolk. They were huddled in small groups, talking low amongst themselves. Thad blinked—the sun had just started to rise, and he had been curled up in a multicolored bit of sunlight shining down from a window made of stained glass.

He was on the floor of his mother's church.

He stretched and stood, one foot absently pawing at the floorboards as he rose. His mother, noticing her son was finally awake, came over to him.

"Thaddeus, thank God!" she exclaimed. "We thought you were never going to wake up!"

"Why is that, Ma?"

"We could not understand how you could have slept with the horrendous noise of battle all around us all night!"

"What battle? What are you talking about?"

"Last night. The Indians attacked the town. You were right. Your friend, the White Bison, came to help. The creature brought the entire tribe of Sioux with it. It was a miracle. They fought the bandits and that captain . . . "

The young man snorted. "I thought all the Sioux were slaughtered. Isn't that what that murdering bastard soldier told us?"

"They were here last night. They all shone with righteous glory. I told you they were God's children, and they saved us." She threw her arms around the young man, held him tight, and then broke away, beaming down at him.

"We have a lot to do, and I'm just so glad you are okay, my darling boy."

The doors opened then, and sunlight streamed into the church. The day already had grown hot, and the stench of death wafted in with the calls of starlings and goldfinches.

The remaining townsfolk of Paradise walked outside, blinking as their eyes adjusted to the morning sun. The buildings were ruined but could be rebuilt. Thad's mother quickly organized the people into groups—some were to look for survivors, others for food, and others for necessary supplies. A few fit horses were found a short time later, and Jasper volunteered to ride to the next town for help. Throughout the day, anything of value, anything that the survivors could use, was brought to the only building left standing, the church. Thad had first cleared the town's well of debris, then helped to organize the supplies for everyone. He and a few injured men made room in the Sanctuary for sleeping. They would all be living in the church for some time.

At lunchtime, the army, along with the Buffalo Soldiers, arrived. They had tools, horses, and additional supplies. The general in charge insisted that the captain behind the marauders was an outright criminal and "got what he deserved."

Curiously, no bodies were discovered. A scouting party had been sent to the Sioux village, and while the encampment was found in tatters, no bodies were discovered there either. All the residents who died during the raid were listed as missing in the official records. Thad's mother organized a prayer service before dinner that evening. That is when Thad slipped away and returned to the caves.

He followed his own path and lit a torch before entering the darkest bowels of the cave. He entered the large cavern with the glittering gem-like outcroppings and stopped at the cave wall that told the story of the White Bison.

Thad spent a few moments looking at the petroglyphs, then he removed a small knife from his belt and reopened the tiny wound on his thumb. He watched the blood well up, then began to draw on the walls. When he was done, he said words no human had ever uttered, in a language long since dead. The swirls of blood on the wall writhed and twisted until they became a very distinct shape.

The shape of a young man.

The blood turned to deep etchings. The carving blinked at its creator, and the creator smiled back.

"You said whomever I wanted, boy. I chose you."

"Why?" asked the petroglyph Thad, etched tears welling in his eyes.

"You forgot the most import part of the legend, boy," said the trickster. "There were *two* gods that fought that day so long ago. The White Bison was cherished and beloved by mankind. The other, the trickster Mica, was coated in white chalk and only appeared in the image of a bison. The legend never mentioned who won, did it?"

Last Sunset of a Dying Age

Michael Burke

PROLOGUE

FRIDAY, OCTOBER 6, 1893, DUSK ARIZONA DESERT

PINK COTTONY TENDRILS slashed the indigo canvas, spilling orange fire across the dusky desert sky. The slap of batwings against the cooling heat echoed in the distance, almost in time with the clop of hooves.

Mick Upstill sat nervously in his saddle and spared a glance upward at the spectacle above, then quickly gazed behind him, pulling his hat low as he did. Nothing.

Over the rise of dunes, he could still see the roofs of some of the taller buildings of Copper City. The brilliant sunset and stark, elemental beauty of the Arizona desert before him did not register on Upstill; his attention was focused on pursuit from the town he had quickly vacated. He thought for certain that someone would be following, or at the very least, raised an alarm. But nothing. Not even a cloud of dust behind him.

The tall rider yanked on the reins, bringing his mare to a stop. Upstill scratched his chin and considered what to do next. Could no one know yet? How is that possible? Concern that he maybe snatched the wrong score waggled at the back of Upstill's mind. His hand darted like a ferret to the pouch at his belly; his long fingers fondled the heavy cloth bag. The weight and metallic clinking there reassured him.

Heading east would be the least expected trail, but he'd have to double back and pass Copper City again and he dared not do that. Mexico was several days' ride to the south, but he'd stick out there like a sore thumb, being as lanky and pale as he was. Plus, he didn't know that much Spanish.

He could light for the West Coast, California, somewhere. Yeah. San Francisco. Upstill had heard it was a bustling city and sure to be filled with rich folks needing to be parted from their coin. He'd need to stop in Yuma on the way and get provisions for the long ride to San Francisco. Thankfully, he had enough money. Upstill fingered the money pouch once more, grinning. Yeah, Yuma was good. If he had to duck into Mexico due to pursuit, it was perfectly located. Best to get moving. It was still a few days on the trail and a posse out of Copper City could be bearing down on him even now.

Spurring his horse's flanks, Upstill headed west, a black shadow on an umber plain.

Thunder rumbled in the darkening sky. Upstill urged his mount to greater speeds, checking the skies for storm clouds. Seeing nothing but deepening colors, he still worried at getting wet and redoubled his efforts.

The sun's tip jutted over the horizon to his right and Upstill felt the temperature drop; he shivered despite himself. He slowed his pace as the horse descended a small incline. It wouldn't do to be found so close outside the city because he took a spill in the dark.

A terrible shriek split the desert quiet, reverberating through the shallow canyon. It was like nothing Upstill had ever heard before. He slowed his horse, searching for the source of the sound.

Coyote? Had to be. They could make some downright eerie sounds.

He worried somewhat about a pack of the critters. He'd hate to have to outrun them out here at night. His pulse quickened as the light continued to fade.

A creaking noise carried across the sandy reach; Upstill pivoted in his saddle and saw the silhouette of a man and covered wagon on a far ridge. They looked to be headed toward Copper City. He couldn't make out any details as they were shrouded in shadow. Still, even at the distance they were, he felt the weight of the figure's gaze. It unnerved him. Curious.

Upstill shrugged. The stolen loot in his purse jingled with the motion, clacking softly in the quiet. As the last echo of shifting coins dissipated, darkness swept upon him, and that same terrible shriek echoed again. His scream lingered long after the ghost of that strange cry departed.

Mick Upstill should have worried about getting dead.

1—Friday, October 6, 1893, Dusk Copper City, Arizona

Leland T. Meade looked up at the sound of thunder. Puzzled, he stared, because the sky outside his window was a deep blue scattershot with the fiery colors of dusk, nary a hint of storm clouds to be seen. The rumble seemed to have come from outside the city limits, somewhere out in the desert.

He stood, straightening his jacket before buttoning it, a habit he had drilled into him since a boy. Always button your jacket when standing, regardless of the number of buttons. Just never fasten the bottom button. Leland had always wondered why have a button that you never use. His father told him that the practice originated in England with one of their kings, one of the Edwards—he couldn't remember which anymore. The man was so fat that he couldn't secure his bottom button so all the men in court followed suit in deference to the king.

Leland stood, moving to the window, and gazed upon the expanse of Copper City. His kingdom. His mind drifted, floating along thoughts of deference and how most everyone here in this burgeoning town owed their livelihoods to him.

There were a few holdouts, obstacles to be sure, but nothing that he couldn't handle easily enough. Copper City needed to grow. He had invested too much into this city.

"Are you still with us, Meade?"

Leland turned from his musings to face the person questioning him. The pastor Orris Wilburne sat rigidly in a high-backed wooden chair, swathed in the black vestments of his station beneath the light ebony cloak he always wore; his right leg crossed over the left in the appearance of relaxation. He gripped the ornate handles of each armrest with long fingers that whitened at the knuckles.

"I am." Leland averted his eyes from the pastor's piercing gaze, focusing on unbuttoning his jacket's top button as he resumed his seat behind the mahogany desk dominating the spacious office. The priest had an uncanny knack for making him feel awkward and unsure. "I thought I heard thunder."

"It's a clear evening. It hasn't rained in almost two weeks. I'm sure it was nothing."

"You're probably right," Leland said, sparing another look out the window.

"You were saying that you had implemented plans to get a railroad line through here."

Leland noted that the priest said this as a statement and not a question as most folks would do to spur an interrupted conversation.

"Yes. I've spoken with the operations and real estate director of Southern Pacific, who assures me he's meeting with the owner of the railway this week. I've told him we're close to striking a deep new vein of copper in the mines and that it would be a very good idea for Southern Pacific to consider having an extension line through here. They will want to get ahead of any competitors and the money they could bring in with investors and passengers would be a great boon as this area marks its second boom. And all of this on the cusp of a new century."

Wilburne steepled his fingers. "Are we ready to discover a new vein?"

"As word gets out and prospectors set up shop, there will be more of a workforce to make that determination."

"So, you're saying the possibility exists there is not a new vein? That could cripple Copper City." Wilburne pursed his thin lips and scratched his hook nose. "A larger population here would fit in well with my plans, Meade, and I would not like to see them endangered by any sin of pride."

"My foreman assures me that signs are good for a fresh strike. A small lode of copper was found, and it looks to go deep. We'll have to go deeper than we have yet, but the reward would look to outweigh the risk."

"I distinctly hope so. A motherlode would certainly bring in potential new parishioners." Wilburne stared past Meade at the swift-gathering dark. Night came up on the desert quickly.

Leland leaned back in his chair, anticipation at the city's—his city's—growth swelled in his heart, overpowering the awkwardness Wilburne always instilled in him. "Don't you worry, pastor. Copper City will get its railroad, it will boom, and there will be more people here than even you will know what to do with."

Wilburne rose in a fluid motion of black cloth. "Indeed. There is much to be done if all this comes to pass. There are many impure sorts still in Copper City and even throughout the greater region. A large and faithful flock can only be of benefit to the good work that I do."

2—SUNDAY, OCTOBER 8, 10:47PM

Darkness shrouded the lone figure rummaging in the alley behind Meade's General Store. Piles of scrap wood, broken rakes, and shovels jutted from an array of burlap bags containing expired feed and other perishables; the stench of rancid cheese hung heavy in the desert air. Several cracker barrels loomed in the gloom like great mounds. The largish figure dragged a rickety cart, its wheels rattling on the uneven ground.

The dark shape leaned against one of the wooden barrels and assessed the sky; clouds scudded across the velvet firmament, chasing the moon. Once the chase was concluded and the moon emerged triumphant, the figure bent to their task, inspecting random pieces picked from the scrap heap. They cast some aside and gingerly placed other items in the cart they had towed with them.

A back door slammed open, causing the wood frame to shake. The impact startled the mysterious figure.

"Get out of here, rag picker!" a smallish middle-aged man stood limned in the doorway. "How many times have I told you, not here!"

Alberta Beggs, the accused, straightened slowly from her task and looked to the strident little man backlit by a flickering lantern inside; his shadow twisted strangely across the ground. "I got a right to be doin' what I'm doin', Zhu Shi." This was not the first time she had clashed with the shopkeeper.

Zhu Shi stepped down from the doorway into the alley, tucking a towel in his belt as he did. "You have no right to do your filthy beggar's work among an honest man's property."

"Ha!" Beggs guffawed. "You ain't that honest, nor is this your property. You is Meade's man, honey-foglin' all us real honest folk. 'Sides, I ain't no beggar."

"I don't care what you are," Zhu Shi snarled. "And what have I told you about calling me by name?"

"Free country. You's lucky I don't call you worse, Chinaman," Beggs bit back.

"You sold up piece of trash. Get out of my alley or I'll scare up Sheriff Bucy." The shopkeep steamed.

Beggs grinned a dirty smile. "Go 'head. I got a right to do this long as I do it during the night. Sheriff Bucy says. I ain't hurtin' nobody."

"Fú zha," Zhu Shi muttered, the Chinese term for 'scum.' Beggs either did not hear him or chose to ignore him. To be honest, she looked forward to these semi-regular bouts with the shopkeep. Hers was a lonely existence, creeping about at night, rats her only regular company while searching others' refuse in alleys and the street, looking for salvageable materials. During the day, she tried selling back what she found to those who could recycle it, making sure to do so early, as businesses opened, so as not to be run off when respectable customers entered. It simply wouldn't do to have someone of Alberta Beggs' ilk to be seen among the fine folk of Copper City.

"Besides, it ain't safe anymore here," Beggs said.

"What are you talking about?"

"I saw a body the other day, out in the desert outside of town. Think it was Mick Upstill."

"Sure, you did," Zhu Shi scoffed.

"I did! At least I think it was Upstill. He was burned up pretty bad being out in the sun, but I could still see it was him. And he looked terribly frightened, scared to death. But I knew it to be him on account'a the spurs on his boots. Because I sold 'em to him."

"You saw a dead body outside of town days ago, and didn't bother to tell the authorities? The vultures would have picked him clean in that time."

"Something . . . unnatural . . . got him. No reg'lar creature would go near. Figgered it best to leave him be."

Zhu Shi laughed a cruel laugh. "More of your tall tales! You're so full of shit. I've had enough, Beggs. Get out of my alley."

"It's true. I gotta protect myself. It could be a Leatherback or Cactus Cat or a Scorpion Man, even. It could be anything. There's more in this here world than we know." She bent to the refuse heap again and pulled forth a two-foot-long piece of wood with rusty nails at the tip. She propped the makeshift weapon over her shoulder.

"Just go, you crazy old woman, and put that down, or I'll have you locked up for being a useless lay-about and danger to others." Zhu Shi turned, pulling the towel from his belt, and wiping his hands as if to signify he was finished with the conversation.

Alberta Beggs did not relinquish her piece of wood, instead choking up her grip upon it. With her free hand, she grabbed the hitch of her wagon and moved off, the one misshapen wheel clunking in the pitted dirt. Her head swiveled from side to side, searching for salvage or danger, one could only guess. The closing shop door echoed in the shadows.

3—Thursday, August 31, 1893, Early Morning, San Francisco Docks

Fog cloaked the San Francisco wharf; buildings squatted like massless toads in the gray coils and the hulks of ships loomed like nebulous sentinels. The salt tang of the Pacific Ocean stung the air, increasing, it seemed, as the sun vaulted the horizon to begin burning off the murk. Fishermen and dock workers shouted, their voices indistinct sounds distorted by the fog, that intermingled with the cries of gulls, creating a dull cacophony of background noise. Occasionally, the shrill whistle of an approaching ship punctuated the din.

The port of call bustled with activity. Thick, hard men went about their tasks, grumbling at the stream of soft passengers boarding great boats to set sail on some adventure or another. Other ships moored or otherwise set sail on missions of commerce, moving in the systematic web of organization adhered to by sailors and port authority; San Francisco was a burgeoning port shipping supplies to and from the northern U.S. coast and Mexico, as far south as Chile, and even ranged as distant as the Far East.

In a gloomy pathway behind several large shipping containers, a pregnant silence bristled with tension fit to explode. It was not an area typically frequented by pedestrians, but two men faced each other across the span of dark space, one man leveling a rust-blued revolver at the other. Voices and activity on the public areas of the dock hummed faintly in the background.

"You've led a fine chase, Ibuki Shibuya, but there's nowhere left for you to run."

The long-haired man at gunpoint stared levelly at the gunman. "I did not consider this to be a chase." He carefully placed his bags at his feet and straightened slowly.

"Regardless of your considerations, you cannot escape your obligations. I am here to assist with that," the gunman said in a heavily-accented tone, gesturing with the revolver. You shirked your duty and must pay the penalty."

Ibuki cocked his head. "I do not recognize your accent or that gun you point. May I ask where you are from?"

"Both I and this revolver are Austrian. The gun is a Steyr gas seal revolver, manufactured this very year and one of only a hundred made."

"It is a beautiful weapon," Ibuki nodded. Austrian? He never imagined his pursuers would be so far-reaching. Nomura must want him badly.

A tiny smile creased the Austrian's craggy face.

"You are another of Yuritaki's bounty men. How sad."

"Sad?" The gunman furrowed his brow.

"Yes. I discharged myself from my *daimyo*—Yuritaki's— service. We disagreed on the meaning of honor. Among other things. I am content to seek enlightenment in the wider world and bear no malice toward him."

The gunman waved his revolver, errant light catching the blue in the barrel, causing it to shine wickedly. "I don't care. Nomura Yuritaki is a high-placed figure in the new Japanese government and completing this task for him while he consolidates his position should net me some very profitable work in the future. He says you shirked your duty and must pay the penalty. The price on your head will establish me quite well in this profession."

The bounty hunter stepped closer. "It's not personal. You're just a loose end." He extended his arm, squinting one eye as he sighted along the barrel. "Goodbye."

Quicker than summer lightning, Ibuki sidestepped and moved forward at the same time. His hair trailed him like a black comet as he trapped the wrist and elbow of the Austrian's shooting arm. He bent the bounty hunter's arm to the side, twisting the wrist.

The Austrian yelped in pain, his cry sounding at the same time as the single shot he managed to get off. Chips of rusted steel spattered in the air as the bullet lodged in a battered shipping container.

Shouts and cries of alarm rose on the other side of the shipping containers as the echo of the gunshot faded. Ibuki knew he had only a minute or two before he was discovered. He spun the gunman around, releasing his arm as he did so, following his trajectory into a steel container with an elbow strike to the man's throat.

The gun fell from limp fingers as the bounty hunter choked and coughed for breath. Before the man's eyes cleared of tears, Ibuki struck him in the nose with his palm, killing him instantly.

The heavy pounding of footsteps on concrete got closer; shouting grew louder. Ibuki retrieved the blue steel Steyr revolver, appraising it quickly before tucking it in his waistband. He hurried to his bags and sparing a final glance at the still form of the bounty hunter, grabbed each of them, and vanished into the maze of containers and buildings, exclamations of shock sounding behind him.

4—MONDAY, OCTOBER 9, 1893, 12:09PM STIFF LANDING SALOON, COPPER CITY

Hollis Bucy bellied up to the pitted, stained bar of the Stiff Landing. After nodding and greeting the handful of patrons inside, he unfastened the chinstrap of his wide-brimmed slouch hat and placed it atop the bar. His belly hung over his belt a little and he tried to get comfortable on his stool but ended up leaning farther forward than he wished. This put a little twinge in his lower back; he felt it every time he moved.

He stroked his black handlebar mustache as he was wont to do when sussing out a problem. Standing up and scooting his hat farther down the right side of the bar, Bucy leaned on his left elbow and settled on a sort of half-standing, half-sitting position on the edge of his stool. The bar supported him, and he could lean closer to the dirty counter, although it sure wasn't all that fine a feeling on his elbow after a while as the pins and needles tingled in his arm.

"Now what, Hollis? You got that look on your face again."

Bucy raised his pale blue eyes to the person who addressed him. Fronnie Camus was the lean, raven-tressed woman who owned the Stiff Landing. She was sharper than he preferred his women, but he understood that not many women owned taverns, much less were allowed inside except as entertainment. But he did appreciate her straightforwardness. Most of the time. Besides, the Arizona desert made everyone a little bit hard.

Fronnie stood behind the bar, holding bottles of whiskey up to the light, inspecting them for bugs with keen dark eyes that hardly missed a thing. "Well?"

"Ah, it's my back again." Hollis adjusted his position, putting his boot on the highest rung of the stool. "You need to get more comfortable seats in here, Fronnie."

"The hell I do. You need to lose that belly. It puts strain on your core. That's why your back hurts. We can't do without an able-bodied sheriff hereabouts."

Hollis shifted his position again, before finally deciding to sit down. He pulled on the edge of his mustache. "Hear tell Copper City might be getting a railroad line," he changed the topic. "That's all I need, more people 'round here. Like I don't have enough trouble with Meade trying to run things."

Fronnie selected a bottle and poured two shots, sliding one over to Hollis. "Wouldn't be half the trouble if you were in better shape."

Hollis rolled his eyes. "Now listen here . . . "

"Don't get your back up." Fronnie drained her glass. "I call it like I see it. You're a good man. A good sheriff. And Copper City needs you. Especially if these railroad rumors are true."

Further conversation halted when the front door violently crashed into the wall. The afternoon sun limned a small, wiry figure standing in the doorway; his features were masked in the shadow of the broad Stetson on his head. Two holstered guns rested low at his hips. But Hollis knew who it was.

Rattlesnake Dick swaggered through the saloon, the cocky grin on his smooth face growing wider as he noted patrons giving way to him. He took the stool beside Hollis and placed his foot on the lower rung of the sheriff's seat. The gunman reached for the whiskey bottle at the middle of the bar.

"How do, Bucy?"

Hollis started. "That's Sheriff Bucy to you." He knew the kid was an instigator, always looking to start something in town. That was just it, wasn't it? He was a pimply, red-headed punk kid. Never been anywhere but the places the dime novels took him, but the kid had a desire for more burnin' a hole in his gut. And he was a fast draw—faster than him. Fronnie's comment still stung, and Hollis regretted the words out of his mouth as soon as he said them. He knew he wouldn't win a confrontation if Rattlesnake escalated the situation.

The red-haired gunfighter laughed as he pulled the bottle to him, untwisting the cork.

"You'll put that bottle back," Fronnie said coldly. "Now." Her dark brown eyes were hard as coal.

Hollis didn't move but kept his hand loose, ready to draw the

Remington revolver he'd had since the War Between the States, if needed. The kid couldn't be fast enough to draw with his attention split. Hollis watched a grin split Rattlesnake's pocked face.

"That ain't very civil of ya, Fronnie. But what should I expect from a half-breed mauk doing a man's job?"

"That's enough, Dick." Hollis stood up; eyes leveled at the gunfighter.

"I'm more than man enough to settle your hash, gump," Fronnie fired back, her mouth set in a hard line.

Before matters could escalate further, the saloon door crashed inward, and Alberta Beggs stumbled through.

Hollis turned at the noise, albeit a little slower than Rattlesnake had reacted, he noted. The kid had whirled at the same instant the door banged with both six-shooters in hand. Hollis rested his hand on his gun butt, flicking the holster strap. The kid was fast.

"Sheriff! You gotta come quick. It's at the schoolhouse."

5—MONDAY, OCTOBER 9, 12:11PM

Norah Callahan descended the rickety steps of the schoolhouse, listening to the creaking timbers split the desert air. She shook her head at the state of disrepair, the motion shaking loose an auburn curl that draped over her face.

"These need to be fixed up right quick. One of the kids could injure themselves," Norah addressed her companion, an older gray-blonde woman, as she tucked her errant curl behind her ear.

The two teachers stood outside the school, staring at the building. "We'll likely have to do it ourselves since Meade ties up funds into getting Southern Pacific to put a line through here. At least that's what I heard at the last town meeting." The older woman leaned in conspiratorially.

"You always have your ear to the tracks, don't you?"

"Best way I know to survive. Those steps, however. That's a different story. Can you swing a hammer, Norah?" the older woman asked.

Norah put her hands on her hips and assessed the stairs with a sharp green eye. "I can figure it out, I think. I mean, we're teachers. That shouldn't preclude our learning new skills." She chewed her lip. "Besides, think of the message it would send the children."

"Luck of the Irish, huh? Oh, honey, the desert hasn't burned the optimism out of you yet. Although if you don't cover up more, you're likely to get a nasty burn with that fair complexion." Norah laughed. "I'm made of sterner stuff. Besides, my fair complexion has not attracted the attention of a decent man since I arrived here months ago. I'm beginning to think such a thing as a decent man is a mythical beast."

The two women laughed, proceeding toward the center of town. "Perhaps we can try that fabled Irish luck at one of Copper City's fine entertainment establishments?"

A strange scuttling noise in an adjoining alley disrupted the women's banter. It sounded like something hard scraping the adobe walls. An odd huffing followed. They stopped.

"What is that?" Norah asked, curiosity lighting her green eyes.

"Likely a dog or cat. Let's go."

Norah lingered, squinting into the alley as the huffing noise increased.

"Oh my God! Norah!" The older woman shoved Norah hard.

Norah screamed as she sprawled into a collection of wooden casks; her skirts caught a sudden hot wind, obscuring her vision. She thought she saw a terrible face before a large shadow rumbled forth from the alley and descended upon her co-worker.

The thunder of tumbling wooden barrels filled her ears, followed by a sudden hard blow to the head, then everything went black.

6—MONDAY, OCTOBER 9, 12:23PM

Hollis Bucy, Fronnie, Rattlesnake, and several other patrons of the Stiff Landing rushed past Alberta Beggs at the sound of the scream, spilling onto the street.

Hollis quickly began directing the crowd. He ordered Fronnie back inside and not leave the tavern unattended and knew he'd pay for that directive by the look on her face. He instructed two others to head to the jail and bring a deputy, and yet another person to the doc's place and have him get prepped for a possible worst-case scenario.

"Rattlesnake, you're with me. Let's go!"

"Yee-haw!" the gunfighter squawked.

Alberta shuffled out of the tavern past Fronnie, whose dark eyes gleamed with anger, concern, and anticipation. The old woman set after Bucy and Rattlesnake.

"What in tarnation is going on?" Meade stood on the front porch of his building, the tallest in Copper City and located diagonally across the street from the Stiff Landing. His arms were crossed against his chest, and he looked for all the world like an angry parent.

"That's what we're off to investigate, Meade," Hollis stated.

"That's Mr. Meade, Bucy. I expect the sheriff of my town to have things under control and to exhibit the proper measure of respect."

Hollis bristled. He gave a sidelong glance at Rattlesnake; the kid bounced from one foot to the other, anxious as all get out to discover the source of the scream and add to a possible body count. All the while, he wore a wide-mouthed grin.

Hollis clenched his gun handle until his knuckles turned white. "I've gotta get going."

"See to it. And I expect a full report." Meade turned on his heel and disappeared inside.

The sheriff ground his teeth and set out at a run toward the schoolhouse, Rattlesnake pacing him easily. He ignored the kid's eyes, knowing the kid wanted to bait him.

Alberta, the old rag picker, followed as quickly as she could.

Hollis and Rattlesnake came upon a gathering crowd just meters from the schoolhouse. The sheriff's eyes swept the scene, taking in everything at a glance. The crowd obscured something on the ground, but he figured it for a body, what with the scream and how people were reacting. People always clustered at some misfortune or other. His pulse quickened when he realized it might very well be Norah Callahan the crowd was looking at and he felt his stomach fall away. He took in a deep breath when he noted Norah a couple yards away, disheveled and being supported by a few townsfolk. She set among scattered casks, and other than being dirty and likely traumatized, seemed none the worse for wear; Hollis let out the breath he'd been holding.

"Move aside!" Hollis yelled to the gawkers.

The crowd parted slowly, letting him through; Hollis sidestepped a puddle of vomit. The hot stink of death filled his nose. Hollis wanted to puke himself when he saw the savaged corpse; he had never seen a body in such a state.

The woman—at least it appeared to be a woman—was in pieces. Blood and gore covered everything in a wide swath around her. Hollis didn't know there could be so much blood in a human body. The torso was . . . chewed . . . in several places. All the limbs were separated from the trunk except for the left leg. At least, he thought it was the left leg; it was so twisted he couldn't be sure. Even the limbs were savaged and half-eaten.

Hollis felt his stomach churn. He backed away, letting the pungent stench of blood not fill his nostrils so much. Whatever had done this was no man.

"Bucy."

Hollis stared at the mutilated corpse in the wet, red dust.

"Sheriff!"

Hollis blinked and turned to Rattlesnake; the kid was crouched in the dirt by an alley mouth. "There's some tracks here. Ain't nothing I've ever seen before but I reckon it's what killed that poor fucker."

"Watch your mouth," Hollis said over the growing mumble of the crowd.

"It's a Leatherback that done this," a raspy voice split the stillness. "I saw it."

Hollis turned to see Alberta Beggs, who had finally caught up to them. The old woman was wheezing and doubled over, her hands on her knees.

"What now?"

"Leatherback. I saw it come from the alley. I was across the street, scavenging. Heard it same as them two teachers there. Well, teacher."

Hollis shook his head, trying to process what Beggs was telling him. "You saw this . . . Leatherback? What in hell is a Leatherback? And what were you doing rag picking in the alley? You're only supposed to do that at night."

Beggs ignored him. "It's a monster. Saw the dead woman there start to push the redhead out of the way before I lit out to get you."

"There ain't no monsters," Hollis rolled his eyes. "It was some kind of animal, most likely." He did his best to restore a semblance of order, directing some folks to fetch a rug or cloth or something to collect the body and its parts before bringing it to the doc. He also saw to Norah and made sure she saw the doc before filing a report with him.

"I saw it, Sheriff. It was a monster."

7–MONDAY, OCTOBER 9, 1893, 1:02PM, SOMEWHERE OUTSIDE COPPER CITY

The stench of decay drifted on the hot desert air, mingling with the smell of his own sweat; it made for a sick, sour odor. Ibuki Shibuya brought the back of his hand across his brow, wiping away the perspiration beaded there. His hair stuck to his cheeks and the back of his neck.

He scanned the shimmering golden-brown wasteland before him for some sign of the smell. Nothing. He blinked his dark brown eyes painfully. Perhaps over the next rise?

Ibuki stopped and pulled a waterskin from inside the vest he wore; he took a small sip, letting some of the warm liquid run through the sparse beard that had sprouted on his chin. He was so tired. It had been over a day since he lost his horse. Two?

The leather reins in his hands burned and Ibuki let them fall to the sand. He had fashioned a litter from his horse's saddle and harness so that he could drag his bags with him. He knew that he was in the western part of America, what he had heard called the frontier. Settlers were increasingly expanding westward as the country grew, so Ibuki expected to come across some sign of human settlement soon. He hoped.

Since his encounter at the San Francisco docks over a month ago, Ibuki had kept a low profile as he headed eastward. Yuritaki held a grudge, and it appeared his reach exceeded farther than he could imagine.

Ibuki supposed his former *daimyo* had to make a showing of it, but he harbored no ill will toward the man. They simply disagreed on the definition of what constituted honor. The world was changing. In so very many ways.

That's why he went ronin.

If only Yuritaki could leave well enough alone. Perhaps losing himself in this fledgling country, he would not be found and eventually his perceived transgression would be forgotten. And Ibuki could live in peace.

He bent to retrieve the reins and his head swam. The lacquered scabbard sheathing his katana was hot and heavy across his back and pulled against his vest and cotton shirt. Ibuki dropped to a knee, the weight of his gun belt dragging him lower. If he could but rest for a moment. He staggered to his feet, reins in hand, refusing to lie down. He considered another drink of water, then discarded the notion. Best to ration what water he had until he spied civilization. Soon.

The flapping of dark wings and the snap of tendons pulled Ibuki from his musings; he trudged over the next incline, boots slipping and sliding in the sand. The sounds grew louder as he slid down the other side. Carrion birds took flight, annoyed at his approach.

Ibuki gazed down at the remains of a man. The corpse's face was miraculously untouched. Ibuki marveled at the look frozen on the man's face—stark, primal fear. No grimace of pain. No wounds on his body beyond the markings of the vultures. He wondered at the man's origins and the fate that brought him to this end. A chill skittered across his shoulders despite the heat.

Ibuki looked away, scanning the horizon. Only more sand and rock. Some larger formations rose from the ground further off. This poor soul had to be from nearby, a day at most. There were no other tracks, just a horse, which he took to be the deceased's own; it must have fled after its owner's demise.

Vulture shadows wheeled in the dirt around the corpse. Ibuki looked up, shading his eyes. He returned his gaze to the horizon. This time, in the shimmering waves of heat, he spied the rooftops of buildings. His heart thumped faster. *How did I not see this before?*

That must be where the man is from. I shall return him to his home. Ibuki dragged his litter closer, and with some effort, positioned the body as securely as he could upon it. He gritted his teeth and stared hard at the buildings ahead. It would be several hours before he reached that town.

Ibuki set a pace with renewed vigor despite a now-heavier burden. Succor gleamed at the end of this path. trudging forth implacably.

A furtive shadow in the corner of his eye distracted him; he was not sure if anything was there or if it were spots in his vision, but Ibuki turned anyway. High on a far rise to his left, Ibuki saw a tall, black-swathed form leading an equally dark covered wagon. They looked to be traveling in the same direction as he toward the town ahead. The strange figure made no sign he noticed him and so Ibuki continued, trudging forth doggedly, followed by wheeling scavengers above, as implacable as he, if not more so.

8—MONDAY, OCTOBER 9, 2:07PM SAINT HUBERTUS RECTORY, COPPER CITY

It doesn't get better than this! Orris Wilburne leaned back languorously, the hood of his omnipresent cloak bunching about his shoulders as he did so; his long fingers pulled at the collar about his throat. The skin on the backs of his thighs slid uncomfortably across the leather seat cushion as he stretched out his legs. Even that small discomfort mattered not in the face of the crescendo of pleasure welling within him. He was denied these sensations by his station; Wilburne knew it was wrong but could not contest the sheer satisfaction of these feelings.

His eyes rolled back as he released and, after a noisy thirty seconds, the prostitute lifted her head.

"Blessings, child." Wilburne twined his fingers in her dark curls.

The woman wiped her mouth, adjusting her bosom. "I can't live on blessings, pastor."

"Of course." Wilburne sat up, wincing as his slick skin pulled away from the leather with an audible ripping noise. He crossed to an ornately carved cedar table and plucked two silver dollar coins from the collection plate; he dropped them in the outstretched hand of the woman as he gazed appreciatively at her gaping bodice. Wilburne marveled at her seeming unconcern with her disheveled dress and recent act.

"Always a pleasure serving the good Lord, pastor." The woman's eyes sparkled.

"Wilburne!"

Leland T. Meade barreled into the rectory chamber, pulling up in surprise at the sight of the pants-less man-of-God and the brunette he recognized as one of the painted ladies who frequented Copper City's saloons.

"It's customary to knock before entering a room, Leland," Wilburne stated; even this unannounced intrusion could not dim his contentment. Ignoring Meade, he turned to the woman. "Thank you again, my child." His fingers traced her jawline, and he watched her swallow hard before smiling.

Wilburne broke contact and watched as the woman brushed

past Leland, who hastily moved aside. The pastor's lip curled in a sardonic smile as he heard her excuse herself with a teasing, "Leland."

Once he heard the outside door close, Wilburne retrieved his pants, draped over the back of the leather chair where he had savored his revelation. He exulted in the discomfort exhibited by Meade at the entire situation. Power had many forms.

"What is it you want, Meade?"

After a moment, Leland collected himself. "Don't you think it's a little careless to, ahh, fraternize with the soiled doves of our fair city? After all, you are a man of power and station in Copper City, with a lot to gain and even more to lose."

"Are you threatening me, Meade?" Wilburne removed the white collar at his throat.

"No. No. I am merely suggesting caution."

Wilburne sensed that momentum had shifted to him, and that Meade had reverted to the submissive mien he typically evinced while in his presence. All bark and no bite. "Caution is to be commended, but at times, there are higher demands upon a man's time. Now what is it that has caused you to leave your ivory tower?" He took note of how Meade bristled at that desultory barb.

"I've received a telegraph from the Southern Pacific Operations and Real Estate Director. Their board has voted in favor of constructing a line through Copper City." The excitement fairly dripped from Meade.

Orris Wilburne smiled. He dragged his fingers through the collection plate, letting the coins clink and tumble to the wooden planks.

9—MONDAY, OCTOBER 9, 3:42PM, COPPER CITY BORDER

The harsh sun beat down like a dry, searing blanket as Ibuki dragged his grisly litter into Copper City. The town had always seemed just over the next rise, but he knew it to be a mirage, an illusion of the heat and his exhaustion.

In all his travels, he had never known such heat, such a desolate landscape. The stories he had heard of the American Southwest rang true—it was vast and could be the death of a man.

Eventually, the dry whisper of wind sighing across the waste melted into the murmuring of voices. Ibuki peered through the sweat-stained strands of long black hair plastered to his forehead to see the shimmering forms of people pointing and staring aghast. He shook his head, clearing his vision. The people were still there, with more arriving from around building corners and stepping onto porches.

He had reached the town. Ibuki halted, laying down his burden. He remained bent over, hands on knees, catching his breath.

"Here now, stranger, what in hell?"

"That there guy has a sword!"

Ibuki straightened slowly, feeling the creak of his joints. He licked his cracked lips, hoping for some small relief, but remained disappointed. He groped for his waterskin and took a long pull. Blinking, Ibuki took in the crowd gathering about him. He did not know who addressed him, but he sensed that the general mood of the people was, if not unfriendly, very wary.

The water eased Ibuki's parched throat somewhat. "*Ossu.*" He slipped into an informal Japanese greeting due to his exhaustion. "I found this man in the desert and thought he might be from here."

"Why that looks like Mick Upstill!" an older man cried, shuffling through a small knot of onlookers. "He disappeared a day or so back."

"So, he is from here," Ibuki said. "That's good. The desert, alone, is no place to die. And where might here be?"

"This is Copper City, and you are not welcome here!"

Ibuki turned to the strident new voice and beheld Zhu Shi pushing through the gathered citizens. "Surely, *watashi no yujin*, you welcome the return of one of your own to make proper allowances for his passing. And would you turn away one who needs water and food?"

"Upstill was a thief and more trouble than he was worth," Zhu Shi said. Assenting grumbles from several of the assembled townsfolk rumbled. "And as for you, begone with you, *guizi.* You are not wanted here and can only bring trouble."

Ibuki bristled at the derogatory term directed at him; he briefly considered drawing his blade but was too tired to retaliate in turn. Besides, he was marginally aware of the tensions between his native land and this man's China, especially as they related to their individual business doings with the America that they both found themselves in. Traveling the world as a ronin, albeit as a fugitive, had taught him much of global affairs and how the world was changing.

He did not think this man spoke for everyone, but Ibuki well knew the power of demagoguery. He had seen evidence of it from the very mouth of his *daimyo*, Yuritaki, before the collapse of Japan's feudal government.

Before he could retort, Ibuki overheard dissenting opinions from the gathered townsfolk. Some of the more generous-natured citizenry believed that succor should be offered a stranger in such straits regardless of his racial origins, and that they were better than this.

"All right, all right! Break it up!"

Ibuki turned once more to behold people making way for a stout man in a wide-brimmed hat stride purposefully toward him. He walked bow-legged and his middle bulged somewhat, but the tin star winking on his vest marked him as a man of authority. Ibuki did not miss the well-worn Remington revolver at the man's hip.

"Sheriff Bucy, this foreigner appeared on the street dragging Upstill behind him," Zhu Shi informed. "Who's to say he didn't kill him and is looking to spread his devil's ways among us here?"

"That'll be enough of that, Zhu Shi," Hollis said with a hard look. "I don't go in much for riling up a crowd and picking at a man's race. You don't make the decisions around here. I do."

Zhu Shi snarled and slunk to the back of the crowd.

"Now, what's your story, mister?"

Ibuki inclined his head in deference to the sheriff. "I am called Ibuki Shibuya. My horse died out in the desert almost two days gone. While walking for civilization, I came upon this man." He gestured to Upstill's corpse. "I then spied your town and figured him from here. I thought to return him here and perhaps take rest before being on my way."

"Ibuki Shoo-boy-ah? That Chinese?"

"I am from Japan. It is an entirely different country." Ibuki sighed. "It is pronounced *Shuh-boo-yuh*."

"I see." Hollis chewed his lip. "Well, first things first. Let's get Upstill over to the doc. He can check you out, too. You gotta have at least sunstroke. Then we can head over to the station house, and you can tell me more."

10—Monday, October 9, 5:11pm, Copper City Jailhouse

Ibuki sat stoically in the hardback chair provided him by Sheriff Hollis Bucy. He had gotten a cursory examination from the city's physician and was deemed fit enough to return with the sheriff to the jailhouse; the doctor gave him some balm for his sunburns and directed him to rehydrate and eat some to regain his strength. As Ibuki sat before the sheriff and the so-far silent red-tressed woman also present, who eyed him intently, he partook of the humble broth and limes offered him. He repeated his tale of before and answered the questions posed to him. Ibuki supposed that making sure his tale was true, made sense considering the circumstances of his arrival and the fact he was a foreign stranger. Be that as it may, he did not care to be without his katana and belongings, but he understood the sheriff's need; Ibuki's eyes tracked to the sword and packs in the corner of the room.

But more concerning to him was the underlying current of fear running through this town, Copper City. He felt it in the street but did not recognize it right away. Now, after a bit of rest and some nourishment, his faculties returned somewhat. That dread fairly radiated from the red-haired woman in the room. It was not dissimilar to the anticipation before a great battle.

"You found your way here to Copper City by accident, by way of San Francisco, and happened on Upstill's body in the desert outside the city limits." Bucy tugged on his handlebar mustache as he reiterated Ibuki's story.

Ibuki set down his bowl of broth and took a glass of water from the desk. He nodded.

"I don't know why but I believe you." Bucy gazed at the man in the chair. "There's something about you . . ." The sheriff continued playing with the edge of his mustache.

"And what about my situation, Hollis?" Norah asked. "I've been sitting here for hours. I'd be as dead as my co-worker if she didn't save me."

Ibuki started at the lilt in Norah's voice. He had not heard such a thing. "My pardon, but I have not encountered such an accent before. Where, might I ask, are you from?"

"I am from Ireland, on the Atlantic coast of Europe. It is quite far from both here and your native Japan," Norah replied.

"Ah," Ibuki inclined his head to Norah. "Thank you. May I ask what it is that happened to you?"

"Well, my friend was killed by some animal . . . "

Bucy cleared his throat. "All right. Let's stay on track here. I don't think Ibuki's situation ties into yours, other than maybe some kind of wild animal killed both Upstill and your friend."

Ibuki noted the brusqueness of the sheriff's interruption. That, conjoined with the woman, Norah, having keenly watched him while the sheriff questioned him, led Ibuki to believe that the sheriff fancied the woman and was perhaps jealous of her directed attention.

"Perhaps I can assist you, Sheriff, in tracking the beast?" Ibuki offered, staring at Bucy.

"Hmmm." Bucy walked around the desk, and stood with his thumbs hooked in his belt. He pursed his lips, sizing up the man seated before him. Making his decision, he said, "I think you may at that. How 'bout you bunk here at the station tonight and we go over some thoughts on the subject?"

Ibuki did not relish the notion of spending further time in the jailhouse, despite his seeming pardon, but he could not truly fault the sheriff's caution.

The station house door opened abruptly; Ibuki rose fluidly from his chair, his hand reached instinctively for his katana, only to grasp empty air. He saw the sheriff note his response to the interruption but could not read the man. Yet.

A finely dressed man of middle years, with cold eyes, strode brusquely through the door. Ibuki did not care for the newcomer.

"What's going on here, Bucy? I understand that this man showed up in town dragging one of our own citizens behind him. Why isn't he in a cell?"

Ibuki assuredly did not like him.

"I say who goes in a cell here, Leland. I've questioned him and determined that he is innocent of any wrongdoing," Bucy stated flatly. "Despite what information you may have received from Zhu Shi."

Ibuki kept his own counsel and continued observing. He liked this man, Bucy; he sensed an ally in him.

"My apologies. I must have been misinformed." Meade smiled, but his eyes glittered like a snake's. He directed his attention to Ibuki. "I'm Leland T. Meade, sir, and certainly you can understand my rash action. I do get carried away when something unfortunate happens in my town."

"Of course," Ibuki said.

"I understand you are visiting from Japan, is that correct, mister . . . ?"

"I am Ibuki Shibuya. I am merely passing through as I travel east." Ibuki inclined his head very slightly in deference to Meade. He sensed this man had power here and was not unlike his former *daimyo*. Best to tread carefully.

"Miss Callahan," Meade stepped to Norah, taking her hand. "I'm so sorry to hear of your friend's demise, but very grateful that you came through the experience. I am positive Sheriff Bucy is on the case." He smiled an oily smile.

Norah pulled her hand away quickly, tucking it behind her back. Ibuki breathed deeply. It seems another man in authority had designs upon this woman. Interesting. He spared a glance at Norah, curious. In doing so, he missed the venom in Meade's response of his appraisal.

Meade straightened his tie and puffed out his chest. "Bucy, be sure to inform me right away when you catch the beast responsible for these two killings. Be it an animal or man." He stared pointedly at Ibuki. "Great opportunities are in store for Copper City, and we can't afford to leave things undone. If you're not up to the task, I'll find someone who can do the job."

11—Tuesday, October 10, 10:09am, Meade-owned Pasture Outside Copper City

The snorting and grumbling of cattle bit through the air, matched only by the pungent odor of manure and hot cow flesh. Large bovine bodies packed close, shuffling about, feeding on corn stalks and the sparse grasses found in the Arizona territory.

Jim walked the perimeter of the fence, shaking his bucket of water into troughs. It was a lousy job, walking around in the heat, tending cattle. Making sure they had enough feed and water. Who the hell tried raising cattle in the desert?

Leland Meade, that's who. Apparently, one could raise cattle in this type of environment. Jim didn't know all from that, but he was a simple man. If it could be done, Meade was likely the one to get it done. The proof was right in front of him. Even if he didn't quite understand it.

Jim continued his slog. Pouring water and dumping feed in the correct troughs. Replenishing from the stores and repeat. It was always the same.

A loud bellow from the far side of the herd disrupted Jim's routine. He looked up to see the cows lurching away from the noise in panic; they pushed closer to where he stood on the fence line. Their deep-throated mooing throbbed in his ears.

Jim looked on in amazement as several heads farther back in the herd vanished in a spray of blood. A strange honking sound drilled through the air and the cows panicked; Jim couldn't make out a thing. The frenzied cattle broke through the fencing, paying little heed to the wire mesh that cut their flesh. Jim backed away in a rush, confused, but not so bewildered as to avoid getting trampled.

Another weird honk split the now-coppery air, followed by a powerful grunting. A fifth cow, by Jim's count, disappeared in a flash of mottled brown flesh and dark blood. He gaped at the cows streaming past him in terror.

Jim never saw the dark shadow that leapt upon him, only briefly feeling the sharp, terrible pain of his torso snapping like one of the dry cornstalks the cows ate.

His feed bucket clattered from lifeless fingers.

12—TUESDAY, OCTOBER 10, 4:37PM, MEADE'S GENERAL STORE

Alberta Beggs glanced at the late afternoon sky, and shrugging, delved into the pile of trash behind Meade's General Store. She waded into the scrap heap to her elbows, rheumy eyes searching for anything of value.

It didn't matter to her that it wasn't yet nightfall in Copper City. To hell with Sheriff Bucy and his ordinance of rag picking only occurring after dark! She wasn't the only picker in town and if she didn't do something to level the field, she'd be sure to get out-picked. The other pickers were younger and faster. Her old bones weren't up to the task anymore. Besides. It was dangerous in Copper City. She knew. She had seen the corpses. Monsters had made their way to Copper City. It was best to get as much work done as possible before nightfall.

Alberta was so engrossed in her thoughts and her work that she did not detect the figure creeping up on her. She straightened triumphantly, if a bit stiffly, holding a crooked iron pan; she scrutinized the utensil with her tongue protruding slightly from the corner of her mouth.

"Too messed up," Beggs decided and tossed it over her shoulder, bending back down to continue her search.

She stopped halfway down when she heard the iron pan strike something other than the ground, followed by an exclamation of pain.

"You filthy trash!" Zhu Shi yelled, rubbing his shoulder. "You nearly hit me in the head."

"Oops. Sorry. Didn't see you there."

"What did I tell you about digging around my store? I don't want you here." Zhu Shi frothed.

"I gotta right to do this," Alberta countered.

"At night!" Zhu Shi said. "It is not night. And even if it were, I forbid you from going through my belongings."

Alberta stepped to the small proprietor. "You can't forbid me from doing anything."

"I can and I do." Zhu Shi snarled and pushed Alberta hard. Not expecting the physical attack, she fell hard on her rump. Tears welled in the corners of her dirty eyes.

"You rag pickers and now that dirty Japanese, this town is going to hell. Copper City used to be a respectable place,' Zhu Shi muttered, kicking dirt at the fallen woman before turning around and entering his store.

Alberta coughed, spitting sand from her mouth. Her eyes stung from anger, embarrassment, and dirt. She couldn't believe that little Chinese bastard! He actually laid hands on her.

She clambered to her feet, gingerly feeling her posterior with a dirty hand. It was sure to be bruised. It felt like she landed on a rock. Maybe it would be best if she headed over to the doc's place.

Sparing a dagger look at the general store's back door, Alberta shuffled out of the dim alley to the street and proceeded the hundred or so yards to the doc's house. The sun sank lower in the sky and people were few on the street. Those that were, gave her a wide berth, but Alberta was used to that. Her profession was not looked upon kindly by many of the citizens here, even though it was legal. She didn't much care what they thought. Ever since Leland Meade took control of this town, good honest folks were in scarce supply it seemed.

Alberta's musings filled her travel time. The sun had dipped below the hills and shadows stretched across the wastes. She stopped in front of the doc's place and considered going in to get checked out. She had money. She could pay the doc for his time. Metal glinted dully in the meager light, emanating from the side of the house. Alberta noted a large crate there; her instincts got the better of her. Let me just see what the doc's thrown away before I go in and see what he can do for me.

Alberta moved to the side of the house and peered inside the wooden crate. It looked like a lot of medical tools, all broken and twisted, crusted over with blood. Dirty, dark rags filled up a lot of the space inside the box. She didn't want to think about where those stains came from.

A movement in the corner of her eye caught her attention and Alberta looked up. The darkening sky was reflected in the glass of a closed window; it was located on the wall to the right of the crate. Alberta furrowed her brow. Strange. Didn't see that before. Why would the doc keep his window closed? As she wondered at that, she thought she saw a shadow move inside.

Alberta moved to the side of the box. If she stood on her tiptoes, she could just peer inside. She noticed the darkness had deepened, creeping up on her, and a chill traced cold fingers across the back of her neck. The sun was nearly gone; the only light in the alley came from another window farther down the same wall she leaned against.

Alberta's imagination reared, her mind conjuring monsters that leaped from underneath the house and out of the crate from beneath the soiled rags. Alberta shook her head, dispelling the phantoms. Aw, it was just the doc inside that spooked me, that's all.

Alberta, still curious, perched up and peered inside the window. It took a moment for her eyes to adjust to the gloom inside, but when they did, they widened in shock; she stumbled back from the sight within, nearly losing her footing as she did. What she saw was more terrible than any creature of the imagination.

She scuttled away, quick as she could. Alberta swore she heard the rumble of thunder.

13—Tuesday, October 10, 3:51pm Stiff Landing Saloon

Ibuki followed Hollis Bucy through the door of the two-story establishment he knew to be a saloon; it was vibrant and clamorous within. They joined Norah Callahan at a battered wooden table in the center of the room. After a much-needed and longer-than-normal sleep at the jailhouse the evening prior, and a welcome visit with a wash basin and straight razor in the morning, he had spent most of the day with the sheriff reviewing the facts of the mysterious slayings that had occurred in and around Copper City.

Ibuki found the lawman to be a man of sturdy character and liked him well enough. He would help him track the beast responsible for the killings hereabouts as he had offered; the hunt intrigued him, and he desired to learn some more of the animal and of the general environment as he had rarely encountered such a place as this desert. He could not imagine the search for the beast to last more than a couple of days. Perhaps in that time, the teacher, Miss Callahan, could assist him in learning more of this country; she was pleasant enough. It would behoove him to make the most of his time while here and the resources available to him before continuing east.

Music swelled from the piano in the corner and several patrons streamed through the door after what Ibuki assumed to be long workdays. He detected several glances shoot his way, blatantly plain and none too furtive, and Ibuki thought maybe word of his arrival had spread throughout the city and people were curious to see the new stranger. He thought it seemed a bit soon to be calling an end to the workday but admitted that he did not know how things ran here in the American Southwest. Ibuki felt the weight of a particular stare; a smooth-faced, red-haired youth at the bar nursed a glass of beer and boldly watched him. Ibuki did not miss the worn, ivory-handled Smith and Wesson Model 3 six-shooters at his hips, nor his easy, relaxed motions.

"In all the time I been here, I can't recall ever seeing such killings. I tend to think it is some manner of animal, as you say, but damn if I know what it could be. There ain't too many big predators around these parts," Hollis stated. "If you plan on helping me hunt down whatever it is, you'll probably need a place to stay. You can't stay at the jailhouse. I'll likely as not need it for official business."

Ibuki nodded, returning his attention to the sheriff. He sat arrow-straight on his hardback chair, leaving space for the scabbarded blade slung on his back.

"Fronnie, she owns this place, has rooms for rent upstairs. Maybe she's got something available?" Hollis scanned the room, and spotting the lean, black-haired woman entering behind the bar from a recessed door, he raised his hand.

After a moment or two of speaking with the bartender, Ibuki watched the woman make her way to the table where the three of them sat. She moved fluidly and with confidence and her dark eyes encompassed everything happening in the room. Ibuki still felt a concerted gaze upon him, but he did not know if it were the youth at the bar, or a particular patron elsewhere in the tavern. He turned to Norah and smiled. Her bright green eyes were narrowed at him.

Ibuki turned when he sensed someone close. The woman Hollis had summoned stood before the table, at the sheriff's shoulder, and he couldn't help but notice that she remained out of striking range even if he drew his blade. Ibuki was mildly impressed; he stood and bowed slightly. He had not entirely forgotten his manners when meeting the lord of a keep, as it were. She eyed him.

"Fronnie, this here is Ibuki Shoo-bya. He's going to stay a spell."

"Please. Ibuki Shibuya," Ibuki corrected.

"You're the man who found Mick Upstill outside of town, right? And you need a room?"

"Please."

Fronnie cocked her head, looking him up and down. She stepped forward after a moment of deliberation and extended her hand. "I'm Fronnie Camus. I own this place. And if Hollis vouches for you, I got a room for you. You mind working for your board?"

Ibuki took her rough, proffered hand. "I do not. Thank you."

"Sit a spell, Fronnie," Hollis said.

"Yes, please," Ibuki agreed. He was intrigued by this woman. He slid his chair over as Fronnie snatched an empty chair from a neighboring table.

"You're Japanese?" Fronnie asked. "And that black scabbard makes your blade a *shinto* katana. You're samurai, right? You're far from home."

Ibuki's eyes widened.

"Damn, girl," Hollis whistled. "How you know all that?"

"Don't call me 'girl.' I been around."

This woman became more interesting with each passing minute. "I am *ronin*," Ibuki stated. "And yes, this is a *shinto katana*."

"What is *ronin*?" Norah spoke up.

Ibuki turned to Norah. Her eyes flicked to Fronnie, then back again. Was there a flash of darker green there? "*ronin* is 'wanderer' in your tongue. I am samurai, as Miss Camus noted, but without a master."

"A 'master?' You were a slave?" Concern speckled Norah's face.

"That's not what a *ronin* is, Norah," Fronnie clucked. Norah stared hard.

"Please," Ibuki interjected. "Samurai were military nobility, beholden to a *daimyo*, what you would call a feudal lord. We were their officers, dispensing duties and defending their holdings." He noted the question lingering in Norah's face.

"Samurai become *ronin* when their *daimyo* dies, or when they fall out of favor with him. When this happens, it is expected that the samurai do the honorable thing and commit *seppuku*."

"Is that . . . ?"

"It is ritual suicide," Ibuki confirmed, triggering a look of shock on Norah's face. "I fell out of favor with my *daimyo*, when the governmental system of Japan changed, and he lost his holdings. His castle was taken by greater forces, and when it appeared he was to be slain, he commanded me to do the honorable thing. I refused."

"Well, I should hope so!" Norah exclaimed. Hollis and Fronnie listened intently.

"The issue was moot as my former *daimyo* survived and found position in the new governmental system. But my refusal brought disgrace to him, and I fell from his favor," Ibuki said. "I believed that the world was changing even before the industrialization of my once-homeland, and the old ways did not hold up to the scrutiny of the present, as evidenced by how Japan has been governed these past twenty-one years. I still believe change is in store."

"There's more to it than that, isn't there?" Fronnie stared hard.

Ibuki took a deep breath. He had rarely shared the details of the past two decades and he was surprised at his own candor. Perhaps the burden of it had become too much over the years or perhaps he knew these people to be true boon companions? "*Hai.* As my once-master has found influence in the new Japan, he seeks to expunge all traces of his former life, and recover his honor, using the resources at his command. That means me. I have been hunted all that time."

"That's a helluva way to live," Hollis said.

"Indeed. I finally came to the American West, land of opportunity, in hopes of greeting the new world I believe awaits us all. And perhaps I can leave the past behind."

"What's all this now?"

Ibuki turned at the shouted question to see the red-headed gunfighter he noted earlier, swaggering his way to their table. He set calmly, watching.

Hollis pushed back his chair but remained seated. "None of your concern, Rattlesnake."

Ibuki detected the subtle shift in the youth's stride when the sheriff moved his chair; how his hand flexed toward his hip and the metal death waiting there. The boy was a fighter and not to be underestimated, despite his age, that much was certain.

Rattlesnake halted a few feet before their table. The scraping of chair legs sounded, as nearby patrons scooted out of the way, creating a wide semicircle, eager to see what would next occur.

"I make my own concerns, Bucy. And I'm concerned at all the attention being lavished upon this here slant-eye. Ain't it bad enough we got that Chinaman running the general store, now we gotta have another one setting up stakes here? When did Copper City become Hong Kong?"

"Begging your pardon, I am Japanese, not Chinese," Ibuki corrected Rattlesnake.

Rattlesnake scrunched up his face as his clear blue eyes slid to the seemingly serene samurai. "My mistake. This dirty Jap. They all look the same."

"That'll be enough of that shit, kid!" Hollis straightened in his chair, only to slow the motion as he stared down the barrel of the six-shooter suddenly pointing at him.

Ibuki tensed, but outwardly appeared to remain undisturbed. The youth was fast.

The piano music stopped.

"You're a spoiled child, Dick. Make your manners!" Norah scolded, her accent thickening. "You should have had a hickory stick applied to your bottom." Her face reddened with anger.

"Ha!" Rattlesnake laughed; his gun hand remained steady. "I got a hickory stick for ya. And I'll apply it to your bottom. I think you might just like it, too."

The flush on Norah's face deepened in color.

Ibuki bristled. He would not abide such crudity. "That will be quite enough." He had taken the measure of this youth.

The .44 caliber six-shooter swung his way, quick as the desert wind; Ibuki did not flinch. "What'd you say, slant?"

Ibuki did not have time to formulate a response, either verbal or physical, as Fronnie clubbed Rattlesnake in the neck with a pistol butt. The youth slumped to the floor with a loud grunt, his revolver still clutched in his hand. Fronnie kicked it from his hand.

Ibuki did not see the weapon on her person as she approached the table, nor did he detect Fronnie moving to attack, concentrating as he was upon the gunman. He nodded, impressed even more with this woman.

"*Petit enculé*! I oughtta take you out back and shoot you with your own gun, Dick." Fronnie hissed at the groggy youth. "Nobody does what you did in my place."

"There'll be no shooting," Hollis called out, trying to regain a measure of authority. "I'll take him in. A night or three in a cell should teach him a lesson."

Piano music started up again, drowning out the shock and crowd's growing speculation on how the recent confrontation would have gone down. The front door of the Stiff Landing crashed inward, halting the music and chatter.

Ibuki whirled, hand at the *katana* hilt over his shoulder. With a swift tick of his eye, he noted Fronnie had her gun up while keeping a booted foot on Rattlesnake's neck.

"Bucy!" Meade shouted. "You should be at the station house, not at a saloon. That's where people expect to find you when there's trouble, for fuck's sake!"

"What's wrong, Leland?" Hollis asked, his nerves raw and irritated. The town proprietor was the last thing needed now. He shifted his attention from Meade to Rattlesnake, stirring on the dusty floor.

"My cattle have been slaughtered. And one of my hands. I want you to do something about this, and now, by God, or you're out of a job!"

14—TUESDAY, OCTOBER 10, 5:16PM MEADE'S PASTURE

The buzzing of flies was a steady hum but not loud enough to drown the wet ripping sounds made by the vultures as they rended their bounty of cow flesh. The stench of death hung over the area like an invisible cloud, choking and thick.

Hollis had never seen such carnage, not even in the War Between the States. Yes, he had seen scores of dead bodies but there was something about this littered field of savaged cows that struck him as more horrific. The way in which their bodies were torn open was unnatural. And the hired hand, Jim, his remains lay in three distinct spots on the red-soaked ground; he looked snapped in half. What in the hell could do that to a man?

The sheriff surveyed the scene, holding his bandana over his mouth and nose. Ibuki stalked the killing field like a grim specter, scrutinizing the corpses, Fronnie nearby, her gun at the ready. Rattlesnake did the same but at a distance from the former pair; he shot dirty looks at them. Hollis didn't have time to drag him in, what with Meade screaming bloody murder, and frankly, the kid was good in a fight. He knew that Rattlesnake was quick and hungry to kill. He'd address the punk's actions at the Stiff Landing another time. Whatever did this, it was better to have the kid with him than against him.

Hollis suspected that Ibuki might also be good to have beside him if things got ugly but didn't know it for certain. He liked the . . . what was it he called himself? *ronin*? And he wasn't sure why, but he felt better with the stranger here. Things were sure to get worse in Copper City before long and he felt he could use a friend when that time came.

And Fronnie. Damn. He knew she'd been around but seeing her handle and take down Rattlesnake earlier—he was still surprised at what he didn't realize about her. All he knew was that she'd been around; she always said that whenever he pried too close. Once, in a rare moment of divulgence, she let loose her father was French, and her mother Mexican, and that they met during the second French and Mexican War. She was young still, not even twenty-five summers, but Hollis felt she lived a life that weighed heavier than her years.

Orris Wilburne had met them there. The dark-cloaked pastor had finished assembling the pieces of the unfortunate cowhand and looked to be delivering last rites. Hollis noted the preacher did not cover his face at the foul stench that hung heavy all about them.

"Well, Bucy?" Leland spat from behind a silk handkerchief. "What are you going to do about this?"

Hollis sighed. "Going to have to get this cleaned up as fast as possible. I count over two dozen head of cattle killed. Hard to tell if it's more because there are so many pieces."

"I won't stand for this outrage. No one gets away with doing this to Leland T. Meade. The people of Copper City depend on me and my cattle."

"You gotta get this cleaned up, Leland, before it draws any more predators or causes a health hazard." Hollis watched a vulture pick at a particularly stubborn bit of flesh; the sheriff did his best to remain calm and not be baited by Meade's sense of self.

"Who did this and what steps are you taking toward tracking them down. No one person could have done this. It had to be a group of rustlers. I don't pay you to do nothing."

"No man did this," Ibuki stated as he and Fronnie approached. "This is the work of an animal. What manner of beast, I know not, but no human hands are responsible for this slaughter."

"Why are we listening to him?" Meade asked, his fervor mounting.

Hollis sighed again.

"I am well-traveled, Mr. Meade. I am certain this is the work of a beast."

"I'm inclined to agree with Ibuki," Fronnie said.

"Now we're listening to the opinions of a glorified barmaid?" Meade shouted. "Is this motley crew what passes for your deputy department?" He directed the barb at the sheriff.

Hollis had had his fill. "Listen, Meade, this is beyond either one of us. I sure ain't seen nothing like this before, and you sure as shit haven't, sitting up there in your ivory tower, so it's good smarts to listen to outside opinions of those who might know better. Regardless of who's giving them." He added pointedly, feeling empowered at voicing some of the frustration he had always felt with the town proprietor, but also knowing it would come back and bite him in the ass. Until that time, he enjoyed the way Meade's face cycled through shock, anger, and helplessness.

"Respect your betters, Sheriff Bucy," Wilburne said, as he silently joined the group, a somber, black-cloaked phantom. "And do not place so much stock in foreign devils."

Hollis bit back a retort. The lean, hawk-like pastor scared him frankly. He stared right through you, and he never blinked, it seemed. And all that pious nature and talk, well he never had any truck with it. Not even during the war.

"The sheriff is correct in one regard, Leland." Wilburne directed his attention at the still-steaming Meade. "This . . . slaughtering ground . . . needs to be addressed. It would not do to have such an unseemly happenstance in light of important pending business."

Meade regained a measure of composure. "Of course. I still want whoever did this in custody."

Hollis exhaled, rolling his eyes as he did so. "I told you, 'tweren't no man."

"Bucy's right," Rattlesnake rolled up behind Meade, all easy confidence and bravado. "An animal did this."

Hollis's jaw dropped, but he quickly closed it. Damn, if the kid just agreed with him. He watched as Rattlesnake eyed Ibuki. Did he see a measure of respect for the *ronin* in the young gunfighter's eyes?

"I don't care who or what did it," Meade said. Hollis noted that the landowner now allowed for the fact it could have been an animal. Was it because a native he had a measure of respect for, and not a stranger or himself said so? "Just get this fixed."

The creaking of a wagon punctuated the charged silence that filled the air. Hollis marked the sound as just over a nearby rise. Someone was approaching.

A distorted shadow preceded the appearance of the physical wagon and rider. The late afternoon sun cast deep hues of orange and red across the blighted field.

A tall thin man, all in black, appearing all the taller for the stovepipe hat perched on his head, reined in the large, sleek horse leading his covered wagon. He swung down from his bench in a fluid motion; the stranger stroked the long, thick mane of the great black horse before turning.

Hollis watched the lanky man stride easily toward him and his fellows. His face was shrouded in shadow. All eyes observed him.

"Greetings, gentlemen. And lady." The stranger inclined his head.

Hollis eyed the man warily. He seemed friendly enough and was so thin, a strong wind could bowl him over. But he was unnerving. Especially to Wilburne, it seemed. The pastor's mouth was set in a hard line. "Howdy, stranger. What can we do for you?"

"I believe it's more in the line of what I can do for you. My name is Mortimer Lutem and I believe Copper City could avail itself of my services."

"Oh yeah?" Peering past the newcomer, Hollis squinted at the lettering on the wagon's canopy: "Mortimer Lutem, Traveling Undertaker" and beneath that, "Tuwile."

Hollis played with his mustache, trying to make sense of that last word. "Two wheel?" Funnily enough, the wagon did only have two wheels. Was it some sort of weird humor?

Mortimer smiled. "It's pronounced 'Two while.' It's an old term relating to my profession."

"Yeah? I thought it related to your cart having two wheels."

The undertaker smiled without mirth. "Droll. It means 'Death is inevitable.'"

15—WEDNESDAY, OCTOBER 11, 2:34PM STIFF LANDING SALOON

In his small, spartan chamber on the second level of the Stiff Landing, Ibuki pulled the two bags from beneath the wood-frame bed and placed them on the thin straw-filled mattress; he combed the contents of the heavy canvas packs, shifting the basketwork shell within as he hunted for what he sought. He was certain that some manner of beast had mutilated the head of cattle despite what the cattle owner, Meade, believed. He did not much care for the landowner—his vain insecurity and his xenophobia—nor the righteous and peculiar priest, but Hollis Bucy was a good man who had shown him respect upon his arrival. Ibuki wished to do the sheriff a good turn and assist him.

Besides, he admitted to a measure of curiosity at the manner of animal which could slay that many cows. It had to be big. He had seen much in his native Japan and in his travels these past two decades plus and valued all that he had learned. Ibuki always appreciated the chance to glean a semblance of how big this changing world truly was. Even if it killed him.

"You're going to need some help tracking this beastie. Whatever it is."

Ibuki turned to see Fronnie silhouetted in the doorway. Her dark hair was pulled back beneath a low-brimmed plain hat, and she wore a cotton shirt tucked into wool pants, tight at the waist and separated by a bright red sash, and loose fitting over her flat-heeled marching boots. Two holsters were strapped to her narrow hips and a knife scabbard protruded from the front of her sash. She held a .44 caliber Henry repeating rifle.

"What are you . . . ?"

"Stow it," Fronnie said. "I know the area and I'm a good shot."

"I do not doubt it."

"I'm coming with. Doesn't hurt to have someone watching your back."

Ibuki was only more impressed with Fronnie. She appeared most representative of the new world that he knew loomed on the horizon. The saloon keeper was different than most of the women he had encountered in his travels; but she was not dissimilar to the *onna-musha*, the faded female warrior class of Japan, last active many years ago. He admired Fronnie's strength of character and seeming prowess.

"We set out before dark." Ibuki strapped scale armor over his shins and forearms, clicking them in place over his denim pants. He affixed a leather hauberk over his loose cotton shirt, tying off the sides. He considered taking his *suji bachi kabuto*, a riveted, multi-plate helm with raised ridges upon his head, but opted to leave it behind.

In addition to his *daisho*—his katana and shorter sword, *wakizashi*—Ibuki buckled a gun belt to his waist. The holster held a .36 caliber Colt Navy revolver. Swinging a bandolier over his shoulder, he glanced at Fronnie; he did not miss the appraisal gleaming bright in her dark eyes. "Let's go."

16—Wednesday, October 11, 1:49PM. Jailhouse

Hollis Bucy leaned back in his chair and gazed at Rattlesnake and Pastor Wilburne. He stroked his mustache, as he often did when considering possibilities. Something was out there, killing folk, and heaven help him he didn't know what it was. He felt caught between two grating stones. He trusted the newcomer, Ibuki—

didn't rightly know why, but he did—and Fronnie backed him. And he'd known her for years. She was sharp and he trusted her instincts. But she didn't have to contend with the politics that he did. She was young and wild, and Hollis envied her freedom.

Meade and Wilburne believed a person, or group, responsible for all the death, and truth be told, Hollis kind of thought so as well. He knew of no such animal native to these parts that could do to people—and cattle—what he'd seen these past weeks. And while they held the power in Copper City, Hollis was beholden to them. As much as he hated it. This was the best gig he'd ever had.

At least Rattlesnake seemed less combative. Ever since Meade's cattle field, he'd been quieter, not as flippant, as much as he pretended otherwise; he seemed spooked. But he appeared willing to listen to what Hollis had to say, which was just fine with him. The kid was good in a fight and whatever was out there, Hollis preferred to have the cocky gunfighter beside him than working against him.

"Did you hear me, Sheriff?"

Hollis refocused his gaze on Wilburne. "I heard you. I'll take Rattlesnake and some men and lead a search myself for whatever killed Jim and all those cattle. This has gone on too long. Meade has plenty of men to get started on cleaning up all those dead cows."

"As you say. As long as all of this is resolved in the next several days."

"Listen, preacher," Hollis said. "I don't much care which 'important people' from whatever railroad company are meeting you and Meade, or about whatever plans you two have to keep getting rich. I just want to police a town with as few problems as possible." Hollis trembled as he snapped at the man of God. He didn't know if it was the adrenaline rushing through his veins or fear at how the dour minister would react to his outburst.

Hollis saw the pastor's eyes light with an indeterminate emotion, but before Wilburne could retort, the door to the station burst inward. Zhu Shi and Alberta Beggs spilled inside, yelling and pushing.

Rattlesnake had both of his six-shooters trained on the two before Hollis had processed what happened. He waved the kid off; Rattlesnake lowered his guns.

"Slow down! What the hell is going on?" Hollis knew these two were always at each other's throats, but he detected an edge of panic behind Beggs' watery eyes. Was she drunk? It wouldn't be the first time.

"It was the doc! He's . . . gone. I saw him and it was terrible. Then, the whole roof." Alberta babbled.

"Slow down, Alberta." Hollis grabbed the rag picker's shoulders. "What do you mean, the doc is gone? When? What did you see?"

Some of the agitation seeped from Beggs' form. She stared hard at Hollis. "I was behind the doc's place last evening and saw a shadow. I looked inside the window and he was . . . "

"What?" Hollis felt Beggs slipping, like sand through his fingers, all weak-kneed.

"He, he was screwing the dead bodies. That teacher from a couple days ago, and . . . " Beggs slumped to the floor.

Hollis, still gripping her shoulders, shuddered; a wave of revulsion burbled through him like sticky molasses. "No." He looked around; Rattlesnake was aghast, Wilburne crossed himself and the sheriff swore he could see the fires of perdition burning in the pastor's eyes. Zhu Shi's face filled with terror, for there was more to this, Hollis could feel it.

"Then the, the roof of his place tore free." Beggs' limbs stiffened, and Hollis let her go. "I ducked down as pieces of it fell around me. I heard thunder and saw . . . something . . . land inside. I swear it was a huge bird."

"Bunk!" Rattlesnake scoffed. "Why'd you wait all this time to tell us?"

"I didn't," Beggs whined. "The sheriff weren't here yesterday after it happened. Heard tell about something with some cattle. And, yeah, maybe I had something to drink after I saw what I saw. I still ain't sure it really happened."

"Cause yer a crazy old drunk."

Zhu Shi interjected. "No. She's not. I saw it, too. So did several others."

"Bullshit."

Hollis straightened. "Shut up. Finish." He directed the last comment to the shopkeep.

"I heard the noise of the roof being destroyed and ran outside, as did several neighbors," Zhu Shi continued. "As I approached the doctor's place, I saw debris littering the ground about the house;

it's still there, as we speak. Then I heard a long scream followed by a bright flash that erupted from the top of the house. The light was so intense, but I saw wings."

"It was the Thunderbird!" Beggs said, eyes wide.

Hollis rolled his eyes. "Jesus. Stop it. There's no Thunderbird. Or Sand Goblin, or any of these other monsters you're so fond of telling everyone about."

"I fucking knew it was more of her crazy bullshit," Rattlesnake went on, shoving one of his guns into its holster.

"She's right," Zhu Shi said. "You know I have no love for her; I find her to be a useless beggar, but I believe her. We both saw the doctor, dead. His face was frozen in great fear."

"The rightful fear of his eternal soul burning in damnation for eternity," Wilburne interrupted. The pastor's face was a mask of seething emotion.

"Even in China, we have a creature similar to the Thunderbird here. It watches humanity and weeds out the immoral."

"Nonsense!"

"It is not!" Zhu Shi fired back. "China is an ancient land compared to your America. We know of many things between this world and the next. Seeing the terror on that face, I certainly believe that the doctor was struck down for some heinous act."

"There is only God," Wilburne snarled. "You dare blaspheme before me? I defy the existence of the supernatural monsters you expound!"

Hollis had never seen the pastor so unraveled. Normally, he was calm, cool, and collected. Certain. Maybe the statue was human, after all.

"The only way to figure out what all happened is to head out to the doc's place," Hollis said. He grabbed his rifle off the wall and made his way to the door, Rattlesnake and the others following.

A few minutes later, they stood outside the shattered remnants of the doc's house. Hollis could hardly believe what he saw. What in tarnation could tear the roof off a building? Everything inside the house was fused into a smooth crystal. Chairs, tables, the tools of the doc's trade, all were fragile glass. Even the vaguely human shapes that rested among the chaos were glass. Hollis strongly suspected those forms were Upstill, Norah's friend, and other recent dead. He trembled as a shiver touched his neck.

Only the doc himself was unchanged. He lay in the scintillating remains of his profession and possessions, with an expression of absolute terror on his face. Hollis had never seen a look like that on anyone's face in all his life. He was inclined to believe Alberta and Zhu Shi. Them two were always at each other, but their stories matched up here, and he could swear the back of his neck got even colder.

"What in the living hell . . . ?"

Hollis turned at Rattlesnake's curse. He had no answer for the young gunfighter.

"It is God's wrath you see before you," Wilburne said. "Obviously, the people hereabouts need to change their ways, lest wickedness overwhelms Copper City, as it did Sodom and Gomorrah." His dark eyes did not blink.

"I don't know about all that," Hollis said, a growing unease blossoming in his heart. "But I do know that we gotta find whatever did this, before it happens again."

17—WEDNESDAY OCTOBER 11, 6:02PM.
MINES OUTSIDE COPPER CITY

The cave mouth yawned dark and deep, promising blackness more frightful than the impending nightfall. Dusky shadows made strange, distorted shapes among the rocks. A low breeze blew, kicking up loose sand, and the skittering of small unseen creatures filled the air.

The low light glinted off Ibuki's drawn katana.

"Well?"

Ibuki looked to Fronnie. Her eyes scanned the surroundings while her fingers drummed nervously along the barrel of her Henry rifle.

"The beast must make its home inside this cave or hereabouts. It is not far from the cattle slaughter and seems a likely locale," Ibuki said. "What is this cave? Do you know of it?"

"Yep," Fronnie replied. "It's an abandoned entrance to the copper mines. This area used to be rich in copper and Meade took advantage of that, buying up the rights. But the mine started to go dry almost two years ago now. Meade started closing dry veins and moving to other parts of the mine, searching for a new strike. Rumor is, he's found a mother lode."

Ibuki sighed. "Man's greed knows no bounds. Something must give. Balance must be restored."

"Yeah? You think his digging around down here let something loose?"

Once again, Ibuki marveled at Fronnie's grasp of the world. She cut to the quick, sure and certain, like a precise sword stroke. "*Hai.*"

"I gotta tell you, Ibuki," Fronnie started, "I've got no desire to head into this mine to hunt some unknown animal. Especially after seeing the condition of its victims."

"Nor do I if it can be helped. I think it best to lure the beast outside where we have the advantage."

"And how do you propose we do that?"

Ibuki smiled. "Sometimes the simplest method is the most effective." He picked up a stone and threw it into the cave mouth. The echo of its clatter drifted outward to the pair of them.

"Ha!" Fronnie laughed. "I like your style, mister *ronin.*"

Ibuki let a grin tug his mouth upward. He retrieved a larger rock and hefting it twice, cast it inside the cave mouth; the crash of rock thudding on stone dissipated as the projectile eventually came to rest somewhere deep inside. Ibuki stepped back, sliding to the left of the entrance, and motioned Fronnie to the right. He searched the ground for a moment and indicated a battered iron mining pan near her. "That there. Strike it against the rock repeatedly in a slow, rhythmic pattern. The different sound should arouse curiosity in the beast in addition to the further stones I toss inside."

"If it's in there," Fronnie said, slinging the Henry rifle over her shoulder and adjusting her grip on the pan.

"Then we move to another cave until we do discover the beast." Ibuki threw another largish stone into the blackness of the cave. Fronnie started banging the pan against the outside wall with one hand, while the other rested on her pistol.

After several minutes of this, they stopped and marked time. Their clatter had spooked the nearby wildlife and the sudden quiet was heavy.

"Doesn't appear this is the spot," Fronnie stated after almost ten minutes. The gloom deepened as night came on.

Ibuki sheathed his blade. "Apparently not. Let us move to another cave."

A peculiar scrabbling sound echoed within the cave, followed by a hiss.

Ibuki drew his katana, the keen steel hissing in return as it whispered free of its scabbard; he assumed a two-handed grip, moving back into his position on the left of the entrance. Fronnie drew both of her pistols.

They waited.

The scrabbling became louder, like claws scraping the stone. Another hiss. Louder.

Ibuki tensed, his knuckles glowing white in the swift-gathering gloom.

Suddenly, a massive dark form erupted from the cave maw, its jaws snapping audibly.

"*Santa mierda!*" Fronnie yelled.

Ibuki slashed downward at the thing's head as it turned to Fronnie. He was aware of her gunfire as his blade rang and bounced back at him; he felt the shock in his forearms. He whirled, clambering up on a loose pile of rocks to regroup, not expecting his strike to yield that result.

"*Tortuga!*" Fronnie exclaimed, still firing. "It's a Leatherback, just like that crazy old rag picker said! But huge!"

Ibuki did not know the term she used but the beast before him was twice the size of a wild boar; it must weigh three hundred plus pounds. It resembled a great *kame*, a turtle. A large, mottled shell, thick with three distinct rows of spikes and raised plates covered its back. A reptilian head with a wicked curved beak extended from the front and stubby, thick legs ending in hooked claws propelled it along the ground.

Fronnie's shots were to no avail. She, too, found higher ground and scrambled quickly to cover.

Ibuki leaped down, rolling to absorb the impact, and gained his feet. He switched his katana grip to his right hand and drew his *wakizashi* with the left. He waded in, making quick cuts to the creature's shell, testing its durability.

The monstrous turtle-thing turned, quicker than he expected, and snapped at him with those ferocious jaws. Ibuki backpedaled neatly.

"Move outta the way!"

Ibuki spared a glance toward the shout. Fronnie had unslung her Henry and opened fire with the repeating rifle, possibly the finest weapon of its kind. He raced to the side, out of her line of fire. Bullets ricocheted off the beast's shell, whizzing by him. He heard a howl.

Turning, Ibuki saw the great turtle moving slower, then come to a halt. Black blood seeped from between some of the shell plates and small wounds on its legs.

The Leatherback snarled from within its shell; it had retreated to safety once Fronnie let loose with the Henry.

"It's vulnerable between the plates of its shell," Ibuki shouted. "But if we can expose its underbelly, I can end this."

"Gotcha!" Fronnie replied. She looked about the desert bowl frantically, formulating a plan on the fly, and recognizing what she sought, clambered down from her perch, and sprinted across the dark plain.

Ibuki saw all of this and, not knowing what she intended but trusting her instincts, moved to the Leatherback. Its head had peeked from its shell, black eyes shining. Sensing Fronnie's pounding steps, it extended its neck farther and swiveled toward her running form.

This was the moment. Ibuki slashed downward across its bared neck with his short sword, ready to follow through with his katana. The *wakizashi* shattered on the armored skin. The beast whipped its massive head around at the failed attack and snapped at Ibuki; he narrowly avoided the creature's bite, but it did catch the end of his scabbard in its mighty jaws.

Stuck, Ibuki drew his Colt with his free hand and fired at the beast's face. The monstrous turtle-thing released its hold and scuttled backward; it lashed its head, spraying blood.

From atop a small ridge, Fronnie threw rocks at the great turtle; they clattered and bounced off its shell. She yelled and screamed at it. The beast turned, angered, and with renewed purpose galloped toward her, much faster than one would believe something of that size—much less, a giant turtle—could move. Its claws clicked as it found purchase on the loose rocks of the ridge. The Leatherback hissed menacingly as it climbed toward its prey.

Ibuki held his sword low and poised at the ready for Fronnie's move. His pulse quickened. He hoped she knew what she was doing.

Fronnie stared hard at the great shelled monster ascending the cairn of stones toward her. Rocks tumbled from beneath its claws, rolling down the hill, barely heard above the noise of its hooked talons and snapping jaws. Its eyes shined death black.

Then, raising her Henry, she emptied it. Not at the

Leatherback, but at its feet, blasting the loose purchase its claws had. The beast bellowed as it scrabbled for a secure perch.

Ibuki saw the monster scratching and clawing before it tumbled down the hill in a shower of rocks and dust. He sprinted forward to meet the beast.

He met the Leatherback as it hit the ground—on its shell. Belly exposed. With a swift, sure two-handed slash, Ibuki opened a gash from neck to hindquarters; a viscous ichor spurted from the wound and a foul stench wafted from its split flesh. The great turtle thrashed and yowled, its motions eventually slowing as its life ebbed; Ibuki stood, splashed in black blood, and listened to its death knell. Finally, it was still.

"That critter died hard," Fronnie said from beside him. Ibuki had not heard her approach. He only had eyes on the beast.

"I believe the killings are over. Sheriff Bucy should be pleased. Let's return to town with evidence of our kill."

18—Thursday, October 12, 3:52am. Stiff Landing Saloon

Raucous laughter interspersed with general hooting and hollering echoed off the walls of the large taproom; the strains of the playing piano were nearly drowned out by the revelry. The lateness of the hour had done nothing to dissuade the number of people present—it felt like most of Copper City was present.

The loud clink of toasting mugs undercut the surrounding noise. Beer sloshed over the rims of the two mugs, spilling on the pitted bar top, the amber fluid mingling with the bright blood staining the wood surface.

Hollis Bucy sat at the edge of the bar, covered in the same bright blood that stained the counter. His hand clutched the handle of a glass mug, but the beer within had gone flat, its head of foam long-since dissipated. He was dimly aware of the merrymaking going on around him, but Hollis could not really take his eyes from the bizarre trophy on top of the bar.

The head of a large bird—easily three times the size of an eagle's skull—festooned in bright feathers was propped up on the counter. Flickering light reflected in the thing's shiny silver beak. Blood still seeped from the stump of its neck where it had been taken from its body and oozed from the bullet holes between its eyes. It was strangely majestic, even in its current state.

"Well, that 'tweren't so hard!" Rattlesnake drained his glass. "Fix me up with another!" He yelled to the man behind the bar; the stranger was not an employee of the Stiff Landing, but he ably slung drinks in the spirit of the celebration.

When Rattlesnake's glass was once again full, he toasted the person nearest him, spilling more beer. He laughed.

"Well done!" Leland T. Meade stated with a flourish; he was dressed sharply in spite of the hour because appearances were everything. The city father moved to the center of the room, the better to be heard and seen by his constituents, buttoning his jacket as he did so. "It's the beginning of a great day in Copper City. A new day! In just a few short hours, when the sun comes up, will also come the dawn of a prosperous new era for the fine citizens of Copper City. All of this could only come about through the brave actions of Sheriff Bucy and his men, who earlier this night, laid low the scourge that had plagued us all in recent days. Let's hear it for Sheriff Bucy!"

Hollis started at the mention of his name but did not reply. The crowd cheered. Someone clapped him on the shoulder.

"I gotta say the killing blow was all mine," Rattlesnake egged on the throng, exultant in the adulation. "Maybe I should be sheriff?"

The crowd whooped. The piano played faster.

Hollis turned to the bright avian head and gazed once more into the sightless eyes that stared out at the festivities occurring around it. He shuddered, thinking such a thing could exist.

It had been many hours since he and Rattlesnake and the others had brought the grisly trophy into the Stiff Landing and Hollis wondered if it would ever stop bleeding. Its blood continued widening about its head and streaming in rivulets down the front of the bar. The crimson flow running the contours of its beak were like the tears of the world, and Hollis felt as if he had taken part in something terribly wrong. The great bird still looked . . . beautiful. Resplendent with promise. But the luster of its feathers did look to be fading.

Hollis managed to pull his gaze from the creature and his eyes found Norah Callahan. She looked sad. As if she'd suffered some great loss. He kind of knew how she felt.

"Fronnie and that slant are wasting their time on some wild goose chase, I tell ya!" Rattlesnake hoisted another tankard, and climbed atop a chair; he swayed, dangerously close to falling, but kept his balance. "Me and Bucy and you lot done got the critter that's been killing folks hereabouts. No clue what the hell they're on about." He addressed members of the hunting party that set after the great bird; the posse raised their glasses in solidarity, although most of the crowd cheered.

"What the hell is going on in my bar?"

Hollis turned to see Fronnie, standing behind the bar, dirty and dusty and carrying a Henry rifle; she was not amused. No one must have heard the back entrance open over Rattlesnake rousing the crowd with his exploits of killing the strange bird.

She whistled, loud and shrill, and most of the crowd noise subsided. "I said, what the hell is going on?"

"Well, there, lady," Rattlesnake interjected, still teetering on top of a chair, "we're celebratin'."

"Get yer ass down," Fronnie shifted the Henry in her grip. "Celebrating what, exactly?" Her eyes scanned the room, marking each of the carousing faces, until finally lighting on the great bird head on top of the bar.

"*Dios mío . . .*" The rifle lowered somewhat.

Rattlesnake remained standing in place. "We're celebratin' my killing of the beastie that's done all the murderin' 'round here."

"Now hold on a minute," Hollis said, getting to his feet.

"Aw, you helped too, Sheriff!" Rattlesnake grinned.

Meade interjected. "This is a good day, Miss Camus. With the dispensing of this . . . creature, the killings have stopped. And with the lucrative future soon in store for Copper City, this could not have come at a more fortuitous time. I daresay your business will be booming in short order and-"

A back door slammed open, quieting Meade. After a moment, a heavy dragging sound filled the silence. Ibuki came into the room, bearing a bizarre and gruesome bundle. Astonished gasps and cries sounded from those nearest to the bloodied and dirty ronin as they saw what he bore; people jostled each other to move away.

With one hand, Ibuki dragged what appeared to be a great saucer that left deep scratches in the wood floor behind it. Inside the bowl were short, thick hunks of mottled flesh, black blood dried upon them; some of the pieces sported clawed appendages jutting upward. A pungent odor emanated from the grisly basin, filling the space.

In his other hand, the ronin clutched a string bag which held a massive reptilian head, not unlike a turtle, but with a wicked beak that looked able to tear a bull in two. "Here be the beast that killed your cattle, Mr. Meade."

A loud chorus of voices erupted at this, as people processed the gruesome remains of yet another strange monster. No one could be heard over another.

"You done got yourself the makings for some turtle soup, there, slant," Rattlesnake laughed. He climbed down from his perch and stumbled over to the bright, bloody bird head. He stroked the crest of feathers atop its skull. "This here beauty is the one responsible for everything."

"You are a fool," Ibuki hissed.

"I don't much care what did the killings," Meade said, "as long as they've stopped. If there were two monsters hereabouts, and they're both dead, all the better. But I'm curious, Mr. Shibuya. What makes you think that thing you hold is responsible for killing my property?"

"Fronnie and I backtracked it from the site of your cattle slaying. We found it in one of the abandoned copper mine shafts not far from your property. Apparently, a tunnel is under your cattle field. The beast came up through that. Tracks match."

"I suspect, Leland," Hollis spoke up, "that your renewed mining probably disturbed the critter." Meade glowered.

"A likely supposition, Sheriff," Ibuki agreed. "I do not know what manner of beast you have there, but this is responsible for killing Meade's cattle and his man." With a slight nod of his head, he indicated the dismembered Leatherback in its shell.

"Now hold on a minute!" Rattlesnake yelled. "How do you explain the doc gettin' killed then? It couldn't be the same creature."

"Wait. The doc is dead?" Fronnie asked.

"Yeah. Roof torn right off his place and everything, but him turned to glass."

"Glass?"

"Yeah!" Rattlesnake said. "How could that thing you have there, rip up a roof? It had to be the thing I killed. It's a bird monster, so it makes sense. Bucy, me, and a posse set out yesterday afternoon to hunt down the critter that done killed the doc. Figgered it had to be something that flew like a bird. Found it after only a few hours nestin' in the mesquites and acacias in the desert outside town."

"It's a Thunderbird." Alberta Beggs said quietly. No one had seen or heard the old woman enter.

"Enough of your fool bullshit!" Rattlesnake scolded.

Ibuki furrowed his brow, stroking his chin. "Have you not noticed the differing manners of death? The man I found outside of town was unmarked, save for an expression of terrible fear. Meade's cattle and ranch hand were torn apart, as if snapped in two."

"As was my co-worker," Norah added, stepping closer to the center of the room.

"Was the doc . . . whole?" Fronnie asked.

"'Ceptin' for being glass, he was." Hollis said. "Except for this look on his face, like he'd never seen something more terrible in all the world."

"Two beasts. Two different killings," Ibuki stated.

The general murmuring of the gathered crowd died down as Orris Wilburne entered the Stiff Landing. The sheer presence of the pastor cowed those around him, and they made way as he strode forward.

"What is happening here? This is a godless hour for such a congregation. And in a heathen-run tavern of all places."

No one answered for a full minute. The weight of the pastor's gaze fell on each person in the room. Everyone shifted uncomfortably.

Meade broke the silence first; he gripped the lapels of his jacket. "Why, Willis, we've rooted out the creatures responsible for the murders that have been occurring and the loss of my cattle."

"Creatures? Plural?" Wilburne interrupted. He stared at Ibuki and the butchered Leatherback in its shell; his gaze ticked to the bag bearing the beast's separated head in the ronin's grasp.

"Why do you carry . . . ?"

"It is *kubi bukuro*, a head bag."

"Savage!" the pastor spat. Then his dark eyes fell upon the candescent and bloody bird head resting atop the bar; his mouth opened and closed but no sounds came out.

"And that is the other creature responsible for the deaths hereabouts," Meade said proudly. "But neither will be plaguing Copper City any longer."

"Do you know what you've done?" Wilburne found his voice.

"Yeah," Rattlesnake burped. "I killed this bird thing that's done killed folks."

Wilburne's eyes bored into Rattlesnake. The pastor trembled, be it with rage or something else, it was unknown. He whirled, and gathering up his cloak, stormed through the crowd, vanishing like he was never there.

"That dude has lost it," Rattlesnake stated.

"Have a little respect," Hollis said. "He's a man of God, and while I don't particularly like him or believe in what he preaches, the man has just had his faith rattled."

"Indeed," Ibuki agreed. "It is a difficult path when one is faced with evidence of something more than what you were led to believe."

A loud crack of thunder shook the timbers of the Stiff Landing and the ground itself seemed to move with the reverberation. Dust drifted in the air, swirling to the floor in little eddies. People shuffled nervously.

An unearthly shriek shattered the silence following heaven's rumble. Fear raced through the room.

Zhu Shi spoke up, his face ashen. "That is the same sound I heard before discovering the doctor. Only louder."

Alberta Beggs nodded in agreement, whimpering as she knelt, seeking refuge beneath a table.

Rattlesnake had his six-shooters in hand, eyes sober. His face was slack. "You mean to say . . . ?"

"*Hai.* It appears the creature you killed was a youngling and its parent has come seeking vengeance." Ibuki said, a grim set to his features.

Dread at the ronin's proclamation swept the Stiff Landing like fire raging through brush. Shouts and pushing increased among the gathered individuals clumped throughout the room.

A burst of wind blew in the front door with a crash; those people nearest jumped at the sudden shock. The tall, lean figure that had appeared spat an oath.

Orris Wilburne stood framed in the doorway, black and shadowed, limned by a roiling sky behind him, looking for all the world like the wrath of God.

Last Sunset of a Dying Age

19—Thursday, October 12, 4:33AM

Ibuki dropped the head bag—it landed with a thud and rolled to one side of its face; the netting that crossed the beaked mouth made the Leatherback look to be laughing. He reached over his shoulder and drew his katana, clenching the hilt until his knuckles cracked. This was the endgame. He knew not what part the man, Wilburne, played in it, but knew he was somehow central to all that had been occurring. Ibuki waited, ready to strike if need be.

Orris Wilburne's black eyes swept the room, cold and calculating, as he stepped inside. Wind howled through the space he had occupied in the doorway, chilling the room, despite the packed space and hot scent of fear.

No one moved. No one spoke. All present watched the pastor, waiting.

Wilburne halted his advance after a half dozen steps. He gazed up at the ceiling and dust still swirling there. "It was all for naught," he stated. "My plans for this town, you people." He spat out the last word like he had taken a bite of something distasteful.

Meade stepped forward sheepishly, straightening his jacket. "Surely, Orris, we can proceed forward. Southern Pacific will be here in days and the influx of prospectors will benefit us both. I don't see why you're so upset."

Wilburne lowered his eyes and skewered Meade with a withering stare. "Avarice is all you see. Greed, hate, and fear are all any of you know. I can no longer save you. Or even myself." The pastor looked askance at the brightly bleeding head of the Thunderbird on the bar top.

"I have grown to desire this prison of flesh and the vagaries that accompany it. But that is not my mission. Your sins have corrupted me. And now . . . " Wilburne's voice trailed off.

"Now nothing!" Meade shouted. "Now that these monsters have been dealt with, Copper City can truly flourish. Especially now. Think of the railroad deal. Get a grip, man!"

Wilburne spared a glance at Meade before returning his gaze upward. "I no longer care for your foolish plans. Or for the denizens of Copper City. All that concerns me now is the purgatory to which you lot have condemned me with your foolish, hateful actions." He reached for the omnipresent cloak at his shoulders, pulling the hood over his head.

When the cloak fell over Wilburne's features, a terrible transformation took place. The pastor shimmered, growing in stature, his limbs changing as dazzling feathers sprouted across his liquid form. His head coalesced, morphing into an immense bird's head, with a great silvery beak like burnished steel; it resembled the smaller one propped in its own blood across the bar. Its glittering eyes were grave as they swept the room of horrified faces.

Even as the transformation occurred, Rattlesnake shook off his astonishment and drew a bead, leveling his guns at the Wilburne-thing; he moved faster than anyone else could react. A testament to his skill, and conceivably, the modern world's impending step into the next century. But not swifter than his target.

Lightning flashed from the creature's eyes, arcing across the distance between them, and fried the young gunfighter in a blue haze. Rattlesnake fell, smoke curling from the blackened hole in his chest—his hands still burned, fused to ivory handles. The smell of cooked meat saturated the Stiff Landing.

The room erupted; screams of horror and panic filled the air. People fled toward the exit nearest them, scrambling over others to make way.

Wilburne glowered at Rattlesnake's smoking corpse, perhaps contemplating on modernization not having yet outstripped the power of fable and the past. "Pathetic."

"Hold," Ibuki barked. "This has all been a great mistake."

Wilburne glared at the ronin, then looked once more at his kin's blood-drenched head, set atop the monument to mankind's sloth. "The mistake is yours. When you struck down my successor. Now I am cursed to an eternity of shepherding your worthless race."

Ibuki began to grasp the enormity of what had happened. He clutched his katana helplessly, wondering what to do next.

"What the hell, man?" Meade stood cowering against the bar. "What are you?"

"I am the Thunderbird," Wilburne answered. "For generations, my kind has watched your slow crawl toward enlightenment and pruned the branches of mankind's tree by eliminating those of low moral fiber. I am your protector."

Meade stuttered, trying to formulate a response.

"But now," Wilburne growled, "I am the last guardian. In a stroke of cosmic luck, you fools destroyed the next generation before it could reach full power. I was to be succeeded, my time at an end. And it would have been good for I have served too long among you, and I have lost my way."

"I begin to see," Ibuki said softly, absorbing the conversation. "It doesn't have to be this way."

"That's the way of the world, Wilburne! Or whatever you are," Meade shouted, anger seizing hold of him. "Progress is the strong stepping over the weak. You profess to be a man of God, some protector of humanity, but you're a man first, regardless of whatever medicine show trick you're pulling off right now. Religion is the tool you use to get your way, whereas I use wealth. You're the same as me."

Ibuki tensed as the cold anger of the Thunderbird swelled like a palpable thing. He averted his eyes, not knowing why he should, just that an instinct directed him to do so. When he dared look again, he saw the town proprietor, who moments ago yelled animatedly about the advance of progress, frozen like a block of unmoving stone.

His eyes grew wider when the Thunderbird flexed its wings and the thunder that emanated forth shattered what remained of Leland T. Meade, cattleman and Copper City founding father.

Those people who had not yet escaped the bar redoubled their efforts in an appreciable panic. One woman tossed a chair through a nearby window. Another wrenched the neck of an older man in a frenzied attempt to reach the door. A man stumbled and immediately curled into a ball as feet pounded over him.

"See?" Wilburne said to no one in particular. "Man cannot be saved. Nor can I now."

With that comment, another thunderclap from the creature's great gleaming wings brought down the house. The Stiff Landing collapsed in on itself.

20—THURSDAY, OCTOBER 12, 5:01AM

As the echoes of thunder and resounding cacophony of the Stiff Landing's collapse faded, those citizens of Copper City still in their beds exited their homes, converging on the remains of the popular watering hole. A massive gray and brown cloud blanketed the surrounding area, choking those near enough and coating everything in a layer of dust and grime.

A bright-hued shadow materialized from the cloud of destruction, striding through the settling chaos as if it were crossing a room. It unfurled resplendent wings as the tumult died down behind it; the creaking of timbers and coughing strangled cries of the wounded heralding the being's arrival. Onlookers retreated before the strange form standing amidst the rubble. Arriving citizens skidded into the backs of their neighbors as those present backed up in uncertain apprehension. Questions buzzed in the air, even as the brave—or foolhardier—drew arms.

Hollis Bucy blinked blood and grit from his left eye as he focused on a soft, gentle hand jutting from underneath a pile of rubble. It was red-smeared, and the fingers were bent awkwardly, but he recognized it, nonetheless. He scrambled over debris to the hand. "Norah!"

Sharp pain stabbed through him as he moved, and he cried out, stars filling his vision. A bone poked through his lower leg. He didn't care. Hollis grunted as he positioned himself to lift rubble. The moans and sobbing of others trapped in the rubble sounded in a hellish chorus about him; in a corner of his brain, he heard Alberta Beggs sniffling about how it was the Thunderbird all along. And he knew the Wilburne-thing was still at-large, but he ignored it all. He had to get to Norah.

His meager excavation efforts were soon helped along when he became cognizant of another at his side. Fronnie. She was dirty and cut up but looked none the worse for wear despite having a building collapse on her. Good ole Fronnie.

"Hey, Hollis."

"Hey." He shoved aside some wood, exposing more of Norah's arm.

"Hollis."

He ignored her. Until he felt her rough hand touch his arm; he stopped.

"She's gone."

Hollis looked blankly at Fronnie. He became aware of a ringing in his ears—had it been there these last minutes? Hollis blinked away the wetness stinging his dust-crusted eyes. He didn't want to believe his friend, but Fronnie never lied to him before. Even when he didn't like what she had to say.

He looked at the arm again and saw that it was just that—an arm. The rest of Norah Callahan, broken neck, and all, lay a few feet away near Fronnie. Hollis swallowed. Peering around, he saw the shopkeeper, Zhu Shi, a broken mess, Rattlesnake's still-smoking corpse, and several other townsfolk he knew. Beggs rocked back and forth amid a pile of snapped timber. The buzzing in Hollis' ears ceased and the sounds of everything around him snapped into sharp clarity. He heard thunder and screams and the crackle of fire. The ground thudded. Looking around, the sheriff saw the back of the thing that was once Wilburne in the street outside, snap its great wings at random; every time that happened, a bright flash followed. He heard people scream every time the light glared.

"Ibuki!"

Hollis turned at Fronnie's alarmed shout; she was no longer beside him. Instead, she stood a few feet away, hesitating on the brink between him, her old friend, and the newcomer, a possible more-than-friend. Hollis grasped all of this in a split-second, that moment, that gulf each person straddles as they march forward in their lives. He drew his Remington.

Hollis liked Ibuki—he was a good man. And if anyone had a chance to save Copper City, he felt that the ronin could. And he would buy him that chance. With his life, if need be. Because what difference did it make anymore? Norah was gone.

Hollis clambered painfully to his feet with the aid of a stout piece of broken wood. He grunted, just another exhalation of pain amid the ruins.

"Bucy! What the hell?"

"Stay back, Fronnie!" Hollis limped forward, ignoring her, mind set; his eyes bored into the back of the Thunderbird. He was dimly aware of Fronnie retrieving her repeating rifle. Of course, that would have been the first thing she grabbed.

With a backward glance, Fronnie hurried beside the sheriff. "You're a fool. I can't let you do this."

"Ain't stopping me, Fronnie."

Hollis halted in contrast to his statement and leaned on his makeshift crutch. He checked his gun's chamber—full. All about him, people died screaming in fire and buildings crumbled in thunder. Wilburne was crazy and looked to take down all of Copper City. His city.

Well, not without a fight.

Hollis opened fire. He heard Fronnie's rifle roar beside him.

21—THURSDAY, OCTOBER 12, 5:23AM

Ibuki scrambled over a large pile of rubble, desperately seeking something. He glanced over his shoulder when he heard his name called. It was Fronnie. He wanted nothing more than to reply—to go to her—but there was something he had to do first. The weight of it crushed him. And it would cost him everything. He could walk away. He had done it before. But no. This needed to be done. No matter what.

He inspected the Colt at his waist only to find it jammed; it was a mere mechanical device and did not survive the debris and dust of the Stiff Landing's collapse. No matter. Ibuki discarded it and moved toward where he estimated his room had been. The echoes of destruction outside the shell of the building rang in his ears. There was not much time.

Ibuki bent to his task, casting aside small hunks of rubble. He picked up a piece of stone that looked like an ear attached to the side of a human head. He shuddered as he recalled Meade's fate and tossed it aside.

There. He had found it.

Ibuki yanked one of his heavy canvas bags from beneath the ruined framework of his rented bed; he rummaged through it. Not this one. He scrabbled for the other bag, finding it farther beneath the bed frame.

He heard the repeating fire of Fronnie's Henry rifle interspersed with the retort of a smaller firearm and he tore through the second bag with raw, bloody fingers. Here.

Ibuki retrieved the Steyr revolver he had taken on the San Francisco docks what seemed an eternity ago; the wood-gripped, rust-blue handgun was intact. He removed his torn leather hauberk and secured the metal cuirass of his ceremonial armor over the dingy cotton shirt he wore and affixed a makeshift *obi*—sash belt—to his Colt bandolier for his katana. Then Ibuki donned the slightly battered raised ridge helm, his *suji bachi kabuto*, the final two components that remained of his former life.

Ready, he strode forward to join his companions, the crack of gunfire ringing in his ears.

Last Sunset of a Dying Age

22—Thursday, October 12, 5:34AM

The thunder of the guns paled before the detonations caused by the Thunderbird's wings and the resultant destruction. Still, the creature turned to see who dared attempt to thwart its vengeance. The sheriff and dark-maned bar wench moved in a widening circle around him, not staying clustered together, thus forcing him to retaliate one at a time. Clever.

As the man moved slower, hobbled as he was by a broken leg, the Thunderbird directed his attention to him; he flexed his great wings, and released a thunderclap that blew Hollis off his feet. He followed the concussive blast with a bolt of lightning from his eyes that consumed the insignificant gnat.

"Hollis!" Fronnie yelled in horror and rage, never ceasing her barrage until the Henry clicked on empty.

The Thunderbird shrugged off the .44 caliber slugs like water droplets. When the rain of lead stopped, he whirled his head, unleashing another bolt of sizzling death from his mad gaze.

Fronnie dove for cover, narrowly avoiding the lightning that nearly stole her life, as it had her friend's. She scrambled to her feet, leaning against the wall of Meade's General Store, panting, and grabbing for more ammunition.

"Fuck you!" she screamed, as she reloaded.

The shattering sound of glass above signaled to Fronnie that she had best move. The unholy Wilburne-thing was tossing thunderbolts all about so that nowhere was safe. Fronnie wondered if anyone in Copper City would survive this day as the building against which she had taken refuge crumbled around her.

23—Thursday, October 12, 5:40AM

Ibuki stared aghast as Zhu Shi's shop caved in upon Fronnie Camus. He wanted nothing more than to go to her, to see if she had survived the collapse. She was the most intriguing woman he had ever met, and he had grown to respect her. Perhaps he could even allow himself to love her. But only if they survived this night. And that could only be determined in one fashion.

"Enough."

The ronin's voice was low but carried across the street to the Thunderbird even over the pleas for help and screams of the dying. The thud of a falling building wall in the dirt seemed to punctuate his simple command.

All motion ceased. If only for a moment.

Ibuki stood, a statue of conflicting eras in his boots and denim jeans with a low-slung holster, his battered cuirass and samurai helm glinting in the light of multiple fires. The bandolier securing his katana scraped across his cuirass; it was the only sound bridging the gulf between him and his foe as he held a level gaze with the supernatural bird creature.

Laughter like a dry wind through a canyon split the stillness. The chill of it lay across Ibuki's shoulders like a shroud despite the warmth of the fires and impending desert heat of the imminent morning sun.

"You dare?" the Thunderbird hissed.

"I only ask that you cease these hostilities. These people have done nothing wrong. It was the actions of a few that killed your kin. There is no need to punish the entire city."

"Are you a fool? Did you not hear me? I am the Thunderbird. It is very much my duty to punish this city and all within it. All of your misbegotten race, if I so choose."

"I do not believe you are in the position to pass such judgment. You must serve in a hierarchy. Your actions would have repercussions," Ibuki stated, trying his best to reason with the creature before him.

"Little man, you would know nothing of the Great Purpose I serve."

"I know that you are a being in pain. And as such, you lash out as any man would," Ibuki said. "You do not have to do so."

"You dare compare me to a mortal fleck such as yourself?" Dawn was only thirty minutes away, but the sky grew darker. "I am so much more, that your simple mind cannot fathom the enormity of my station. Thus, you do not comprehend why you must die. Why you all must die."

"I cannot allow that."

The Thunderbird laughed again. The wind howled louder.

"I challenge you for the life of this town," Ibuki declared. He drew his katana from its lacquered scabbard; it made a soft hiss.

"I cannot be slain, you foolish man. Only a new Thunderbird

can supplant me, allowing me to return to whence come the Four Winds. But your once-ally, by some astronomical chance, slew the new Thunderbird before its powers fully manifested. My rest is denied."

"You will rest when you cease this path."

A cloudburst broke above, and a pelting rain fell. The fires still burned despite the deluge. With a mighty roar, the Thunderbird unleashed a coruscating blast of galvanized death from his glittering, pain-maddened eyes.

Ibuki began moving as soon as he noted the sky darken further, but even he was not swifter than lightning. The electrical discharge glanced off the metal of his chest plate, launching him in the air. He landed in a heap several feet away as he watched the reflected bolt strike a smoking pile of rubble.

He lay still for several moments, wriggling his extremities, feeling the needles of sensation returning to his fingers and toes with painful pricks. Ibuki listened to the sounds of further destruction. It appeared that the Thunderbird considered him dealt with.

Ibuki was not yet done. No.

He clambered painfully to his feet, and drawing the Steyr gas sealed revolver, aimed carefully at the back of the Thunderbird's skull. He despised such a cowardly attack, but this was a foe greater than him. And so much was at stake. *Hai*, he had seen the ineffectuality of gunfire against the creature but perhaps Hachiman, the war god of Japan, would smile upon him this day.

Ibuki hesitated. The only way to reach the Thunderbird was to appeal to its human nature. Was it not the man, Orris Wilburne? That way had to be the path to its defeat.

"I said enough!" Ibuki yelled.

The great avian creature turned. Ibuki fired one shot, catching the otherworldly bird of prey in its shoulder, and knocking it off balance.

Wonder swelled in Ibuki's mind when the Thunderbird stumbled, but he swiftly holstered his gun and spread his arms. "I only wish to speak to you man to man. That shot was merely to get your attention."

"I am not a man." The Thunderbird lashed out with a massive wing, pinions sprouting metal edges as it swung close. Ibuki deflected the killing blow with a two-handed parry of his katana. The clangor of steel rang through the gloomy pre-dawn air.

Ibuki retreated several steps in a sideways defensive posture, sword at the ready. "You are the clergyman, Orris Wilburne. You are aggrieved at the slaying of your kin. This is a natural, human reaction."

The creature straightened, then rose slowly, levitating a foot above the littered street. "No. I am the Thunderbird." It glowered with baleful dark eyes.

Ibuki blinked his wet hair from his eyes and maintained his gaze at the magnificent being before him. "I am truly sorry for your kin. I do not lessen your grief, but your actions must stop. Be the man I know you to be."

"You do not listen." The Thunderbird sighed. "Wilburne is a mask I wear. I. Am. Thunderbird."

Ibuki widened his stance, seeking balance, as the ground beneath his feet quivered, seemingly ready to split open in fury in response to his foe's wrath. Perhaps he was wrong?

The Thunderbird descended. "Since you are fixated on my mortal guise being my true nature, I will satisfy your folly." He shimmered like a half-buried jewel as he raised a bright-hued wing over his wickedly curved beak.

The lean, hawk-like pastor Orris Wilburne appeared before the ronin; he wore the vestments of his station as Ibuki had always known him. His hands were behind his head as if he had just doffed a hooded cloak. His black eyes sparkled cruelly.

The rain let up a little, but the sky remained overcast.

Ibuki peered deep into those passionless black orbs. He saw no trace of human emotion there. No man could be this . . . empty. He did indeed face a higher power.

He breathed in. If his moment was now, then so be it.

Ibuki moved like summer lightning. He slashed at the throat of Wilburne and then again across his torso with a back slash. He drew his Steyr and fired twice. Straight at each eye.

He had challenged this creature for the life of Copper City. Ibuki believed that mankind deserved its chance to better itself on this, the cusp of the twentieth century. The world was growing so fast, there was so much to learn.

It was wrong that innocents pay for the mistakes of a few. Copper City had to be saved. If only to have a chance to deliver on the promise of greater things. And his chance was now.

Wilburne still stood, scarlet tears streaming from the holes in his head. Ibuki gawked as he saw those black eyes regrow in the pastor's head and heard the jelly of those reformed orbs squish as they settled in place. Crimson still ran down his gaunt cheeks, commingling with the blood that stained his preacher's collar at his now-repaired throat. "I cannot be slain. I told you."

Quicker than a match head sparking, Wilburne snatched Ibuki's katana by the blade, unmindful of the sharp steel, and reversing it, thrust the blade through the charred, lightning-blasted spot in the ronin's cuirass.

Ibuki gaped as the Steyr revolver fell from his fingers. He heard his katana clatter to the hard ground, even as his legs flowed like water, and he slumped to the dirt. He looked up at Wilburne and thought, perhaps, he saw a change in those boundless black eyes.

"You were correct, in a way, Ibuki Shibuya," Wilburne said, gazing down at the fallen ronin and the widening pool of blood beneath him. "I am a man. Insofar as human foibles influenced my time as Orris Wilburne. I thought that guise to be crucial to my mission but the longer I spent as he, and with the contact of such as Meade, I became tainted, corrupted."

Wilburne knelt. "I grew to love the mortal pleasures of the material world. I admit to losing the path. My mission, my way, returned to me when I saw my successor struck down. This created an inner conflict within me. Seeing your heart these final moments has helped put things in perspective somewhat." He straightened and stepped over the dying ronin as if he were not there.

"I have much to reflect upon." Wilburne pulled up his hood and vanished in a swirl of dark wind.

Dawn came as the morning sun broke through the swiftly dispersing storm clouds now that the Thunderbird had departed. Ibuki heard the crackling of dying fires and settling ruins as he gazed upward at the brightening sky, wondering. The tentative sounds of citizenry stepping forth from their hidey-holes and speculating on the seemingly long dark night of their souls intruded on the clarity of his reverie. He gasped a ragged breath.

"Ibuki!"

And then, Fronnie, bruised and bloody and dirty, was beside him; she gently removed his helm and cradled his head. Her dark complexion filled his vision. "I am dying."

"No."

"*Hai,*" he coughed. "It is good. Copper City is safe, I think. And you."

Fronnie stroked his cheek with rough fingers, but he had never felt anything so soft.

"Yesterday must give way to tomorrow. It is the reason I became *ronin.* The remnants of ages past and the unseen wonders of the world are always with us. But the folly of man must never outreach his wisdom. Take this lesson, Fronnie Camus, and live your life to the fullest. After death there is nothing. Make me this promise, my friend."

"I promise."

Ibuki smiled as his vision grayed at the edges, blurring. Fronnie was the last thing he saw.

24—Thursday, October 12, 6:30am. Dawn

The familiar creaking wheel of a certain covered wagon reverberated through the fire-slashed vestiges of Copper City. The noise rang like a harbinger of things to come. Be they for the better or not, who could say?

Fronnie recognized the odd lanky shadow of the man from the cattle slaughtering ground. The traveling undertaker. She eyed him as he hopped lithely down from his high seat and petted the long dark mane of his black horse. Fronnie watched him as he observed the destruction surrounding them and the survivors that trickled outside, scurrying about in varying efforts to either scavenge or rebuild.

Mortimer Letum ambled through the carnage and turmoil toward her. The stovepipe hat atop his head bobbed somewhat with his steps; she did not think it looked comical, more like he was an apocalyptic horseman striding through a battlefield. He halted some feet from Fronnie, sparing a lingering glance at Ibuki on the ground beside her.

"Looks like you have your work cut out for you," Fronnie said, gathering herself, still struck by the loss of Ibuki, Hollis, her business—her home these past few years. She shivered. It was all beginning to settle in, but she still did not know why the tall, thin man in black made her so uneasy.

"Yes," Lutem agreed. He looked away from Ibuki's lifeless form and stared hard at Fronnie.

"Death comes for all."

Last Sunset of a Dying Age

Epilogue
Dusk. Time and Place Undetermined

Slashes of brilliant orange and coral pink tinged the full indigo clouds above. The desert sky was a vibrant glimpse of the beauty that nature proffered every day in all manners, if only one would see.

A lone observer scanned the colorful firmament. He trudged across the desert sands, unmindful of the radiant sun and heat and elements. He did not shield his eyes as he gazed upward at the heavenly panorama; he merely took it in, dispassionate.

Orris Wilburne continued his trek through the trackless barrens. He had spent much time in this harsh wilderness. Much. He had awaited his successor all this time but there had been no sign, no portent, if another were to ever come.

He did not know.

He may be the last. It was not right. He had served his time.

Wilburne had mused long and hard on humanity and his own follies. In all that time, he had not found any concrete answers. All he knew for certain was that he was likely cursed to eternity.

A distant roar filled his ears and he looked up. Fading sunlight glinted off another one of those metal canisters high, high above, marring the natural perfection of the color-streaked expanse. He did not think that they should fly so high.

Wilburne halted, and drew his cloak over his head, passing from sight as if he were never there in the first place. Only the silhouette of wings on the sand marked that anyone or anything had been there in the arid wastes.

The shadows vanished even as a rumble of thunder echoed in the heavens.

The End?

Not if you want to dive into more of Crystal Lake Publishing's Tales from the Darkest Depths!

Check out our amazing website and online store.
https://www.crystallakepub.com

We always have great new projects and content on the website to dive into, as well as a newsletter, behind the scenes options, social media platforms, our own dark fiction shared-world series and our very own webstore. If you use the IGotMyCLPBook! coupon code in the store (at the checkout), you'll get a one-time-only 50% discount on your first eBook purchase!

Our webstore even has categories specifically for KU books, non-fiction, anthologies, and of course more novels and novellas.

Subscribe to Crystal Lake Publishing's
Dark Tide series for updates, specials,
behind-the-scenes content, and a
special selection of bonus stories
- http://eepurl.com/hKVGkr

About the Authors

James A. Moore is a best-selling fantasy and horror author. He has been nominated for the Bram Stoker award four times and won the Shirley Jackson Award with Christopher Golden for editing *The Twisted Book of Shadows* anthology. He has written novels for the Aliens franchise, Buffy the Vampire Slayer, and Predator, in addition to writing extensively for the award-winning World of Darkness roleplaying games and for Marvel Comics. His original fiction includes the Blood Red series of vampire novels, the Serenity Falls Trilogy with his recurring anti-hero, the immortal Jonathan Crowley, the critically acclaimed Seven Forges series of fantasy novels and the grimdark Tides of War trilogy and, with Charles Rutledge, the Griffin & Price series of crime-horror novels, along with multiple standalone novels, including the Lovecraftian *Deeper*, and weird western *Boomtown*. He is an active member of the Horror Writers Association, where he was both secretary and vice-president for multiple terms, the International Association of Media Tie-In Writers, the International Thriller Writers Association and Science Fiction and Fantasy Writers Association. He is the author of over forty novel length works in horror, fantasy, science fiction, crime and westerns. He writes for adults and young adults.

R. B. Wood is a recent MFA graduate of Emerson College and a writer of speculative and dark thrillers. Mr. Wood recently has appeared in Crystal Lake Publishing's *Shallow Water's* anthology, as well as online via *SickLit Magazine* & *HorrorAddicts.net,* and in the award-winning anthology "*Offbeat: Nine Spins on Song*" from Wicked ink Books. Along with his writing passion, R. B. is the host of *The Word Count Podcast*—a show of original flash fiction. His second novel, *Bayou Whispers* was released by Crystal Lake Publishing in 2022.

R. B. currently lives in Boston with his partner Tina, a multitude of cats, and various other critters that visit from time to time.

Michael Burke is a lifelong fan of fantasy, science fiction, and horror, propelled into these realms at a tender age when he discovered his father's cache of pulp novels. A passion for comic books soon followed. His mother fostered a love of westerns and 50s science fiction movies.

While deciding what he wanted to do for a living, taking jobs that ranged from the music industry to promotions to security to construction to pharmaceutical, Michael co-founded the award-winning comic book and collectible store, Comicazi, in Somerville, MA in 2000.

When not sorting the comic stacks at work, Michael can be found at home, releasing the hobgoblins of his mind into short story form. He has been published in *Whetstone:Amateur Magazine of Pulp Sword and Sorcery, The Horror Zine, Northern Frights, Witch House*, and the 80s-themed anthology, *Totally Tubular Terrors*.

He lives in Massachusetts with his wife, Angie, who kindly supports and encourages his writing and comic book passions. He is a lucky man. Now, if only he could decide what he wants to be when he grows up.

Crystal Lake Publishing's most popular anthologies:

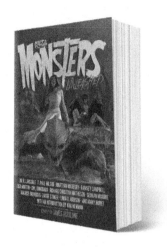

Readers . . .

Thank you for reading *West of Hell*. We hope you enjoyed this 2nd book in our Dark Tide series.

If you have a moment, please review *West of Hell* at the store where you bought it.

Help other readers by telling them why you enjoyed this book. No need to write an in-depth discussion. Even a single sentence will be greatly appreciated. Reviews go a long way to helping a book sell, and is great for an author's career. It'll also help us to continue publishing quality books. You can also share a photo of yourself holding this book with the hashtag #IGotMyCLPBook!

Thank you again for taking the time to journey with Crystal Lake Publishing.

Visit our Linktree page for a list of our social media platforms. https://linktr.ee/CrystalLakePublishing

Our Mission Statement:

Since its founding in August 2012, Crystal Lake Publishing has quickly become one of the world's leading publishers of Dark Fiction and Horror books in print, eBook, and audio formats. While we strive to present only the highest quality fiction and entertainment, we also endeavour to support authors along their writing journey. We offer our time and experience in non-fiction projects, as well as author mentoring and services, at competitive prices.

With several Bram Stoker Award wins and many other wins and nominations (including the HWA's Specialty Press Award), Crystal Lake Publishing puts integrity, honor, and respect at the forefront of our publishing operations.

We strive for each book and outreach program we spearhead to not only entertain and touch or comment on issues that affect our readers, but also to strengthen and support the Dark Fiction field and its authors.

Not only do we find and publish authors we believe are destined for greatness, but we strive to work with men and woman who endeavour to be decent human beings who care more for others than themselves, while still being hard working, driven, and passionate artists and storytellers.

Crystal Lake Publishing is and will always be a beacon of what passion and dedication, combined with overwhelming teamwork and respect, can accomplish. We endeavour to know each and every one of our readers, while building personal relationships with our authors, reviewers, bloggers, podcasters, bookstores, and libraries.

We will be as trustworthy, forthright, and transparent as any business can be, while also keeping most of the headaches away from our authors, since it's our job to solve the problems so they can stay in a creative mind. Which of course also means paying our authors.

We do not just publish books, we present to you worlds within your world, doors within your mind, from talented authors who sacrifice so much for a moment of your time.

There are some amazing small presses out there, and through collaboration and open forums we will continue to support other presses in the goal of helping authors and showing the world what quality small presses are capable of accomplishing. No one wins when a small press goes down, so we will always be there to support hardworking, legitimate presses and their authors. We don't see Crystal Lake as the best press out there, but we will always strive to be the best, strive to be the most interactive and grateful, and even blessed press around. No matter what happens over time, we will also take our mission very seriously while appreciating where we are and enjoying the journey.

What do we offer our authors that they can't do for themselves through self-publishing?

We are big supporters of self-publishing (especially hybrid publishing), if done with care, patience, and planning. However, not every author has the time or inclination to do market research, advertise, and set up book launch strategies. Although a lot of authors are successful in doing it all, strong small presses will always be there for the authors who just want to do what they do best: write.

What we offer is experience, industry knowledge, contacts and trust built up over years. And due to our strong brand and trusting fanbase, every Crystal Lake Publishing book comes with weight of respect. In time our fans begin to trust our judgment and will try a new author purely based on our support of said author.

With each launch we strive to fine-tune our approach, learn from our mistakes, and increase our reach. We continue to assure our authors that we're here for them and that we'll carry the weight of the launch and dealing with third parties while they focus on their strengths—be it writing, interviews, blogs, signings, etc.

We also offer several mentoring packages to authors that include knowledge and skills they can use in both traditional and self-publishing endeavours.

We look forward to launching many new careers.

This is what we believe in. What we stand for. This will be our legacy.

Welcome to Crystal Lake Publishing— Tales from the Darkest Depths.

Made in the USA
Monee, IL
30 September 2022

14385243R00089